CHINABERRY SUMMER
Riverton, Alabama 1947

By

HARRIS GREEN

Bloomington, IN   authorHOUSE™   Milton Keynes, UK

AuthorHouse™
1663 Liberty Drive, Suite 200
Bloomington, IN 47403
www.authorhouse.com
Phone: 1-800-839-8640

AuthorHouse™ UK Ltd.
500 Avebury Boulevard
Central Milton Keynes, MK9 2BE
www.authorhouse.co.uk
Phone: 08001974150

First published by AuthorHouse 8/30/2006

ISBN: 1-4259-4303-9 (sc)

Printed in the United States of America
Bloomington, Indiana

This book is printed on acid-free paper.

Lyrics from "Dance Ballerina Dance" are used with the kind permission of Michael Sigman of Major Songs and Molly Hyman of Harrison Music Corporation.

ACKNOWLEDGEMENTS

The author is indebted to the Big Canoe Writers for the extensive reading and numerous suggestions they made toward the novel's improvement. He also thanks Annelise Green, Carsten and Leigh Green, Teague Beck, Ben Blackburn, Sonya Smith, and Alan Gibson for reading the whole manuscript and providing feedback.

Table of Content

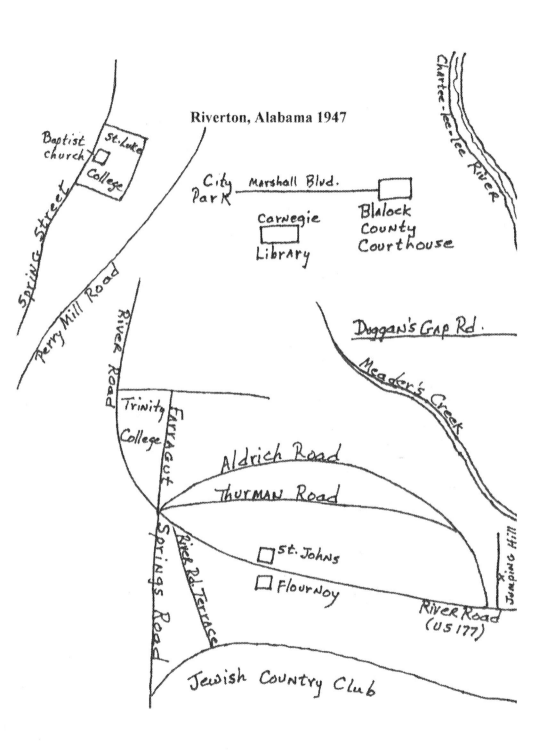

Riverton, Alabama 1947

THE SOCIAL ORDER
OF RIVERTON

IN 1947, RIVERTON, ALABAMA WAS typical of small Southern cities. Blacks lived either in a segregated area of town or in a shack out in the country, where it was not uncommon to see on the highway a black man in bib overalls and a slouch felt hat driving a dilapidated wagon pulled by a mule.

What some called "Niggertown" was in the far western part of the city. Covering several city blocks, it was originally a slave quarter for the servants of merchants, lawyers, doctors, professors, and other city dwellers. By 1947, the neighborhood had everything from shacks to nice brick apartments to even nicer brick or stone houses owned by the black middle class. On a Sunday morning one could hear glorious gospel music pouring out of the doors of Spring

Street Baptist Church, on the western edge of the campus of St. Luke College. Some Riverton whites enjoyed driving to the church on Sunday morning and parking next to the curb so they could listen to the music.

In the northeast sector of the city was the Ramar district, populated by textile workers employed at Blalock Mills. Some lived in the company housing built in the late nineteenth century. Others lived in the better houses in the nearby neighborhoods. In their spare time the workers went bowling at Lois Lanes or took in a minor league baseball game at Barkley Field. They drank lots of beer--even the women--and played poker. The only thing that separated them from northern factory workers was their racism.

In northern mills and factories there was plenty of racism and a lot of *de facto* segregation, but one still might have a black foreman at work or a black classmate at school. In the South, segregation was *de jure,* which meant there was strict legal segregation of the races, and the mill workers enjoyed far more rights than did the black doctors downtown or the black professors at the black college. Therefore, any resentment the mill workers might have felt toward the more privileged citizens of Riverton was mitigated by their feelings of superiority to all black citizens. There was no labor union, so the workers by and large had no say in the running of the mill. But the working conditions and wages were pretty good, so there was little strife.

In the River Road area southeast of the city were the white middle class neighborhoods. The most prominent of these surrounded Trinity College and Riverton Country Club, which bordered the college on the east side. During WWI the country club was in the country, but the growth of the city put the club just inside the city limits. Other nice neighborhoods stretched westward from River Road to Perry Mill Road. Among the houses in these neighborhoods were a few that belonged to the "first families" of Riverton.

These families traced their ancestry back to the founding of the city in the early 1800's by fur trappers who worked the Chartee-lee-lee River, a Creek Indian name which means "to come together." The white settlers later shortened in to Chartee (Shar-tee). After a few years of trapping, some of them decided to get married and settle down. They were drawn to the rich bottomland they found on this particular stretch. They built cabins on bluffs overlooking a great bend, where the river was wide and shallow, and gleaming sandbars on the opposite shore invited swimmers on a hot day.

Over the next hundred years the city grew westward, and beautiful houses standing majestically on the bluffs replaced the original cabins. The flu epidemic of 1917 drove the bluff dwellers away. Medical authorities at the time feared that the swampy areas in the river basin might have something to do with the disease, so the stately old houses were closed up, and most of the inhabitants moved to the neighborhoods near Trinity College.

By the early nineteen thirties some of the houses had been torn down and others made into apartments or duplexes. By 1947 the original settlement was one of the poorest sections of the city.

Boys and Summer

"Who's got uh inner tube?" slurred Graham, while picking at a piece of pear skin between his teeth with a twig.

"I'm sure we got one in the back of the garage," said Todd as he tossed the remainder of his pear into Mrs. Donovan's canalilies.

Barefoot and wearing nothing but short cotton pants with elastic waistbands, the boys had just passed through Mrs. Henry's yard and helped themselves to a large pear each from her tree.

With a coolness of a combat-seasoned veteran, Blake said, "I've still got a pocket or two from last year," but he looked much too young to be credible. "But we need a few more. Either of y'all got any old shoes?"

This conversation continued until all of the components of the slingshot were accounted for--rubber strips from inner tubes, the tongues of shoes, and shoelaces. The boys then went their separate ways to gather the materials and meet in the tree house later.

It was June 1947. School had been out only a few days, and between the April air of early morning and the August air of afternoon the boys concentrated on nothing but summer adventure. On this particular day they talked about the soap box derby and selling Kool-Aid and "funny books" and maybe Burpee seeds to buy Red Ryder B-B guns. As the sun rose higher and hotter, the talk turned to swimming holes and swimming pools. Of all the activities they talked about that morning, the one they returned to most often was the chinaberry battle they so looked forward to. The battle had become an early summer tradition in the neighborhood, and getting to fight in the battle had become a rite of passage. Little boys who fought honorably became big boys and got invited to join the River Road Rangers.

"Did you get the pockets?" Graham asked as Blake climbed the 2x4 slats nailed to the tree.

"Yeah, I found one from last year and I got two more from some old tennis shoes Janie don't need no more."

"Well, I got half uh inner tube, so we got plenty of rubber. Looks good, too. See here." Graham stuck the dusty rubber tube in his face just as Blake reached the last slat and flung himself onto the wooden platform the boys called a tree house. Made of different kinds of wood, of different lengths, some painted, some split, the tree house had a distinctly homemade look. Despite the look, and despite the splinters, the boys loved it. All three of them could lie side by side, high in the big chinaberry tree, and look out over the back lot that would soon become a battleground.

Graham Flournoy, ten, was a little tall for his age, but thinner than he should be, a trait he inherited from a long line of skinny Flournoys, whose only fat arrived in middle age and took up residence on their stomachs. He had mousy brown hair and light brown eyes. The most reflective of the three boys, he was generally deferred to as the leader.

Todd, not quite ten, very ably filled the role of lieutenant. Blond, short, stocky and highly energetic, Todd was excitable, and when in the grip of an idea or passion his face would redden and his blue eyes would flash.

A few months younger than Todd, Blake had very short "cotton-top" blond hair. Because he wore a perpetual frown, he looked older than he was.

Speaking almost in a whine, his brow deeply furrowed, Blake asked, "Do y'all think Murray will bring his mawk orange cannon again this year?" He gave the impression that he hoped one of the other boys would say, "Nawww, it's too dangerous!" But the others said nothing. The three boys lay there, side by side on their stomachs, their chins resting on their folded arms, contemplating what they had witnessed the year before when they were too young to fight.

Murray Austin was leader of the Ramar Renegades, a group of boys from the Ramar neighborhood about a mile northeast. Murray was fourteen and tall and fat. He managed his band mostly by intimidation, since he was older and bigger and louder than the others. His "cannon" was a motorcycle inner tube he had cut in half and tied to the frame of a six-foot floor fan he found in the trash behind Curtis grocery. With the fan and casing removed, there was a frame that vaguely resembled the Y of a slingshot. Murray had tied the cut ends of the tube to the frame with bailing wire. The boys then found some lumber and constructed a heavy 2x4 frame around the base to hold it steady. Then, to make the contraption mobile, they mounted wheels to the four corners of the base. They got the wheels from an old Western Flyer wagon they "found" in somebody's front yard.

Suddenly sitting up and crossing his legs, Blake said, "Maybe we better get some more wood and build some sides for the tree house. Do either of y'all know where we can get some lumber? I think if we nail some boards on the side so that they stick up, we could have somethin' to duck down behind when Murray shoots a mawk orange at us."

"That ain't gonna do a bit of good, Blake," groused Todd, as he sat up, a little upset at his friend's lack of savvy. "Don't you remember what the mawk oranges did to that plywood in Clark's fort last year? Clark and Richie don't need your advice about building the fort this year! Let them worry about it!"

But they couldn't. All three boys fell silent as they recalled the devastation. What were called mock oranges in the region had nothing to do with oranges. They were about the size of a grapefruit but much heavier, being full of pulp and a thick, sticky white substance that sweated through the lumpy green skin. The largest could weigh close to two pounds. If any of the boys had been hit by one of them, he could have been seriously injured—-and the boys knew it.

With the burden of this worry resting on their stooped shoulders, the boys sat there in the moist, mid-afternoon heat, looking like three little shoemakers, as they strung together the shoe tongue pieces, shoelaces, and rubber strips to make their slingshots. The finished product employed a foot-long length of red or black rubber, about an inch wide. One end of the strip was attached to the center of the shoelace, whose ends were attached to the sides of the shoe tongue.

After finishing two good, strong slingshots each, they headed to Meader's Creek, a half-mile away, to practice shooting sticks as they floated downstream. They also hoped to see a turtle or snake, either of which would make a more interesting target.

THE BUTCHER BIRD

AS THE THREE BOYS STROLLED along the dirt road, kicking up dust with their bare feet, the air was tinged with the musty-sweet smell of magnolia blossoms. A large wild tree grew close to Meader's Creek, two hundred yards away, and was full of dinner-plate size blossoms.

"Smell that magnolia?" said Todd. "Next Christmas we're not paintin' <u>any</u> leaves. Last year we spent all that time paintin' those leaves gold and silver and hardly sold any. Whose bright idea was that?"

The boys had gathered the green, glossy leaves and made Christmas decorations out of them. Five inches wide and a foot long, the elliptical leaves made an impressive addition to a table display. For an even more dramatic effect, the boys painted some of them gold and some silver. They soon learned that the housewives preferred the plain green ones.

The boys' inventory also included wild holly, with its bright red berries; mistletoe clumps, with their milk-white berries; and pine boughs with cones. Traveling door to door they were able to sell the clumps for 25 to 75 cents an item, so by the time school let out for the two-week holiday, they had made $19.35 for Christmas presents.

"Boy! I sure would like to see a snappin' turtle!" said Blake, while shooting at a blue jay off in a pine tree. Forming a big hoop with his arms, Blake exclaimed, "That one Clark caught was a monster! His shell wuz as big as a garbage can top!"

"Yeah! That's a good idea!" said Todd, as he punched Blake in the shoulder. "If we see one stick up his head we'll throw you in to go get 'im for us!"

"You're not throwin' <u>me</u> in!" Blake whined while rubbing his arm and frowning. "Graham and me are goan throw <u>you</u> in. You're always talkin' so brave!"

"Nobody's goan throw nobody in the creek!" said Graham. "Those snappin' turtles are dangerous. Don't you remember when Clark touched his tail with that pencil and he threw his head back and snapped that pencil in two? He could bite off your fingers!"

The boys were intimately acquainted with the creatures of the fields and woods, but they rarely saw a snapping turtle, and then just its large head and pointed nose sticking out of the water. A more common turtle was the terrapin they would see in fishponds. It was not unusual to see a dozen sticking their heads out of the water, or see several of different sizes sunning themselves on a log sticking out of the water. The shell of the largest of these was only about six inches, but the shell of a snapping turtle could be eighteen inches in diameter.

A land turtle they saw from time to time was the Eastern Box Turtle. They always picked it up to watch it pull in its head and feet and close up its shell. Then before putting it down they would check the amber-colored bottom of the shell to see if anybody had written something there. Two years before, Todd found one that had "RT+MW 1939" written on the bottom in black ink. He carried the turtle all over the neighborhood showing it to everyone he saw. Since then the boys had been on the lookout for another turtle messenger. They enjoyed speculating as to who had written the message and how far the turtle had carried it.

They knew not to bother snakes. Blalock County was home to the eastern diamondback rattler, the copperhead, the coral snake, and the cottonmouth. Anytime they played near water they were on the lookout for the cottonmouth. Once when they were running in single file along the bank of Meader's Creek, Todd rounded a bend and suddenly saw a large snake coiled up in the middle of the path. It was sunning itself in a patch of sunlight shining through the Spanish moss canopy. Close by the snake were walnut husks that had fallen from the black walnut tree overhead. Todd saw all of this in a split second and even imagined the round walnut husks were snake eggs. But he was running so fast he couldn't stop and just leaped over the snake and kept running. Graham rounded the bend and saw the snake strike in the direction of Todd, but he couldn't stop either. He too just jumped over the snake and kept running as fast as he could. Blake, as usual, was bringing up the rear and as he rounded the bend he saw the white mouth turned toward him, and he leaped three feet over the snake's head and slightly twisted his ankle when he landed but ignored the pain as he ran after his companions. Later, Todd and Graham said they thought it was a cottonmouth and Blake confirmed it was when he mentioned the white mouth.

"If I see a cottonmouth today I'm goan take off his head!" bragged Blake as he drew back the pocket of his slingshot and shot a piece of gravel at a pine sapling fifty feet away. He grazed the two-inch diameter trunk of the pine.

The boys continued down the dirt road to Meader's Creek without a care in the world, occasionally taking a shot at a fence post or a bird in a tree. Just before reaching the woodlot and creek Graham saw a "butcher bird" impaling a tiny mouse on a barb on the barbed wire fence. They could hear the mouse squealing. Officially known as the shrike, the bird looked like a miniature mocking bird, with the gray feathers and black markings. The shrike also had black markings around its eyes that resembled a mask, so its burglar's attire, together with its gruesome eating habits, had convinced the boys that the butcher bird was in league with the devil.

"It's a butcher bird! Get 'im!" yelled Graham as he shot a piece of gravel, hitting the barbed wire close to where the bird sat. The other two boys quickly fired but not before the bird fluttered away to a hawthorn bush behind the fence line. They ran over to inspect the mouse, which was still squealing, even though the barb was buried in its stomach.

"Oh, No!" cried Blake, clutching at his stomach as though he could feel the pain himself.

"Damn!" said Todd. I'm glad I'm not a mouse!"

Graham just stood there, transfixed by the gruesome scene. After standing there for several seconds, not knowing what to do, he stooped down and picked up a stick from the ditch and flipped the mouse off of the barb on to the ground. It lay there in the grass trembling and still squealing--but not as loudly as before. The boys looked from the suffering little creature to the butcher bird waiting patiently, close by in a persimmon tree, staring at the boys through its black mask. All three boys felt sorry for the tiny mouse but sensed that the bird would win in the long run. It was just nature's way.

As they entered the woodlot they lost interest in their slingshots and became pensive. Walking along the path in the heavy shade of the hardwood trees, keeping an eye out for poison ivy and sumac, they discussed how cruel nature can be. They tried to convince themselves that the butcher bird was just doing what comes naturally, but they couldn't dismiss the mental image of the warm, soft, innocent mouse suffering a horrible death.

"It says in the Bible that God's eye is on the sparrow," said Blake. "But why doesn't He watch out for mouses, too?"

"Graham Bishop Flournoy, where have you been? I've been worried sick about you! I was just about to call the poh-leese!"

Anna Flournoy was predisposed to melodrama and used it to full effect when Graham or her other children upset her. A slightly heavy-set woman in her late forties, Anna tried to conduct the affairs of her family in such a way that they could enjoy the delicate pleasures of "gracious living," one of her pet phrases. Graham had left the house shortly after breakfast that morning and now it was getting dark.

While pulling at his left ear and staring at the floor, Graham replied, "Me and Todd and Blake were down at the creek, Mama. We didn't know it was gittin' so late. Did everybody eat already?"

"Of course we <u>have eaten</u>, hours ago! And you're lucky there's anything left!" she spat. "I ought to wear you out and send you to bed hungry!" She wore a light cotton apron, which displayed a bright assortment of flowers. Her auburn hair with gray streaks over her ears was drawn back into a bun. Several delinquent grey hairs played about her neck. While rubbing her hands on the apron, she jerked her head toward the kitchen sink, "Go wash those filthy hands and get your plate out of the oven!"

Todd and Blake met a similar fate at home, but all of them felt it was worth getting in trouble, for they had finished their slingshots, got in some target practice, and plotted their strategy. But even though they were bone tired, they couldn't fall asleep right away. They kept seeing the tiny mouse squealing and trembling, and the devilish butcher bird in the persimmon tree, watching through its black mask, patiently waiting for the boys to leave so it could finish its job of killing and eating the little mouse.

RUTH ST. JOHN

WITH A GNARLED, ARTHRITIC FINGER, Ruth St. John parted her yellowing curtains. In a quaking voice, she asked, "Rachael, what do you think those roughnecks are up to now? They're standing around the Flournoy mailbox. They're holding those awful rubber things, those...slingshots. Last week I saw one of them shooting rocks at a cardinal-—a beautiful <u>cardinal</u>, mind you! I went out on the porch and yelled at him. He ran off... somewhere over there."

Rachael had been dead four months, but Ruth couldn't break a lifelong habit of talking to her sister. She was all alone in the house now, with only an occasional visit from the priest or one of the deacons at St. Luke Episcopal, or perhaps from her only living relative, Cousin Bea. Even though she was alone, she always dressed formally each morning. She usually wore a dark blue or gray, ankle-length dress, usually with a lace collar. Her gray hair would be gathered at the back into a bun, held in place by a silver or whalebone comb. The darkness of her dress would be relieved by a string of pearls. Anybody who didn't dress nicely each day, even if she didn't go out, was "white trash" in her book.

Ruth lived across the two-lane highway from the Flournoys, in the Aldrich home, which was a neat, white frame house with a wide porch across the front. In the wide but shallow front yard, mature water oaks and sugarberry trees thrived. At the right of the house a dirt and gravel driveway disappeared into a yard where the grass was too splotchy to be called a lawn. To the right of the driveway stood a rotting wooden pump house with a rusted tin roof and an ancient windmill. The whole structure was smothered by wisteria vines whose clusters of purple flowers sent out a delicious scent in the early spring.

Being as old and venerable as it was, and occupying the apex of the hill as it did, the house dominated all other houses on the hill, but in a reserved sort of way. You rarely saw any activity there. The stillness and dignity of the home place made it seem a monument to the past.

Remington Aldrich, Ruth's grandfather, built the house in the early 1850s. Like every other farmer in the area, Rem grew cotton, along with other crops, but his was only a small operation of about two hundred acres, which included the entire hill and some of the flatland below. He kept a few dozen slaves and was reputed to be a kind master. When supervising their work he would sit tall in his saddle at the edge of a field, the reins held loosely in his gloved hand. Being a big man, he felt his presence-- boots, breeches, short coat, and Stetson, high on the back of his horse Chestnut- - would be enough to keep discipline among the workers. He rarely spoke to the slaves, but when he did he spoke softly and never threatened them. He prided himself for not speaking harshly to his slaves, let alone striking them.

During the late 1850's and early 1860's the abolitionist news in the *Riverton Press* stirred up a lot of angry debate, but Rem chose to stay out of it as much as he could. His wife, Dancer, felt it was not her place to speak out on the issue, but she would speak to him after they went to bed. During the winter of 1861, the atmosphere in and around Riverton got so tense that when they tried to fall asleep they couldn't. They would just lie there looking at the dancing shadows on the high ceiling, cast there by the banked embers in the fireplace. If they lay there long, Dancer would slide her hand over and take Rem's to give it a reassuring squeeze. If she spoke, she spoke softly. Dancer understood that it was her place to support her husband, but she felt that "support" implied sharing her opinion.

One night in late January, as they lay there, she whispered,

"Rem, I hate to see your brow so furrowed all the time. You look older than you are."

"It's the times, Dee," Rem whispered. "Everybody I know is looking older. These are perilous times. If the South secedes, and the North declares war on us as rebels, there's going to be a lot of bloodshed. I worry about you and the girls. I worry about the plantation if all our slaves are set free. And what would happen to the slaves? What would happen to Aunt Polly?"

Dancer gave a big sigh and continued, "Don't worry about me and the girls. We want to help you, not give you more worries. Maybe the Abolitionists are right. When I'm with Aunt Polly, I feel like I'm with my mama. She is so sweet and kind I sometimes think of her as white. And how can a white person be somebody's property? I know she's not white, but what do you call all those darky children fathered by their masters? I know officially they are slaves, but I have trouble with that idea."

"I can't afford to be philosophical, Dee. I've got to be practical. You know I don't abuse slaves, and I won't permit anyone else to abuse them, but I need them to operate the plantation. If some other way can be worked out so that we can free the slaves, then I'm all for it."

Her contact with slaves was restricted almost entirely to the women who came up from the slave quarter to help her with household chores, the "house slaves." The slave quarter was a collection of shacks down the hill known as The Patch, so named for the vegetables that grew there in patches. When the women came up to the house in the morning to work they would generally bring something from The Patch to use in the cooking that day.

Her contact with the "field slaves" was mainly during such times as "hog killin'," which was always just after the first frost in the fall. Like her mother and grandmother before her, she and a couple of the black women would be on hand when the hot intestines and organs came pouring out of the strung-up, gutted hog. They would gather up the organs and take them to the kitchen where they would become chitterlings and "sweetmeats." Whether they be black or white, according to slave superstition, the women who helped with the "killin'" had to be screened to make sure they weren't pregnant, because meat handled by a pregnant woman would be "spiled."

Dancer had been served by slaves her whole life. In fact it had been Aunt Polly who suggested her name to her mother when the aged black woman with snow-white hair had commented on the newborn girl having "dancer's legs." Dancer had never personally known anyone who abused slaves, so when she would hear of a runaway or a whipping she was almost as shocked and dismayed as were her slaves.

She thought of them as child-like, gentle people who needed the whites to take care of them. But unlike many whites during that time, she thought of them as human, equal to her in the eyes of God but very dependent on her and the other whites to take care of them. She had no problem with blacks getting an education if their lives could be made better, and would help a slave learn how to read, despite the laws prohibiting slave literacy. She did not, however, believe that blacks could ever acquire enough knowledge to handle freedom and would always be dependent. If she had lived in the north and could have known about someone like the ex-slave Abolitionist, Frederick Douglass, she might have become an Abolitionist herself. But the information she received through newspapers, books, the pulpit, and gossip all reinforced the pro-slavery position.

Although pragmatic, Rem was a thinking man and would have done well at the university in another life. When they talked at night, he and Dancer were in basic agreement that it might be possible one day for the slaves to be free. But it wouldn't happen any time soon. Therefore, Alabama was correct to insist on its state's rights.

When the war broke out in the spring of 1861, Rem was called to serve as captain in the Ninth Alabama. Dancer was left with two daughters to raise while taking care of the farm. The day he rode off to join his regiment, the ground under the windmill was covered with dried wisteria petals, which well suited her somber mood.

His letters to her were sporadic but as upbeat as he could make them, so she lived in low-key dread day after day. She turned the managing of the house over to Emma, the senior house slave, and spent most of her time supervising the work in the fields. In addition to the crops they normally raised, they had added a few acres of sorghum to make syrup under a contract with the Confederacy.

In 1863 she learned that Rem had been killed in a skirmish during Lee's retreat from Gettysburg. For the rest of her life the sight of the dried wisteria petals in the spring reminded her of the day Remington left, and once again she would see him sitting tall on Chestnut's back, loping down the dirt road to Riverton, out of her life forever.

Soon after the war, Dancer met and married Richard Blalock, a veteran whose wife had died of typhoid fever. Dancer's older daughter, Beverly, and her new husband joined the other Confederate ex-patriots who moved to South America rather than live in the Union. The younger daughter, Charlotte, some years later, married a haberdasher, Tom St. John, and raised two daughters in the city.

By the 1880's the harsh realities of Reconstruction had

ended and Riverton was thriving. Dancer and Richard decided to subdivide the farm into house sites of 100 X 300 feet along the highway, now known as River Road, and along Aldrich Road, which formed the northeast boundary of the farm. They kept fifty acres behind the house for a few cattle, an orchard, and a large vegetable garden. Richard used the money raised from the real estate sale to invest in various businesses in and around Riverton. When he died in 1901, he left Dancer enough money to live modestly but comfortably, which she did until her death in 1905.

After the death of Dancer, Charlotte and Tom moved from their house in the city to the farm, where they lived until their deaths in the 1920s. Their two daughters, Ruth and Rachael, never married and continued living in their grandmother's house. They inherited enough money to live as their grandmother had, modestly but comfortably. Rachael died in February, 1947, at age 73. By June Ruth had adjusted well enough, but without her sister to talk to she developed an interest in the outside world—-especially those "roughneck" boys she saw through the window, who made a habit of using her yard as a thoroughfare.

The Popsicle Boy

In Blalock County, the more genteel middle class whites, such as the Flournoys and the St. Johns, never used the word "nigger." Nor did they ever refer to grown black men as "boy." The children were taught to address a black man as "Jake" or "Willie" —-whatever his name happened to be. They were to refer to him as a "colored man." However, the gentility went only so far, in order to preserve the caste distinctions. The children learned never to say "Yes, ma'am" or "No, sir" to blacks, as that would give them too much status. They also learned that a black woman could never be a lady in the full sense of the word. Nevertheless the children were taught to respect and to "mind" the blacks who cared for them. White children were comfortable with the dual status of adults in their world because virtually all blacks they encountered were clearly of African origin. Not only that, but they were all poor, wore crude or hand-me-down clothing, and were illiterate or nearly so. The children's comfort with the system would have been seriously disturbed if the children had been able to interact with the articulate, cultured, and well dressed black doctors and professors in Riverton. Both consciously and unconsciously on the part of these genteel white parents, the children were not put in contact with that class of black people.

Graham was taught "genteel" attitudes, Todd and Blake somewhat less so. Two other Rangers, Mister and Ralph, were allowed to use "nigger" at home, but Lonnie's parents, originally from Pennsylvania, would not permit the use of that word. They also did not understand the prohibition against calling a black "Mister" or "Mrs."

Murray's parents, although working class, were "genteel" in their attitudes because of Sara's upbringing as a Jew in Detroit. Butch Avery was Murray's best friend and a fellow Renegade. Butch's parents were both racists through and through, so the term "nigger" was used casually in his home.

On one particularly warm and humid afternoon, the three boys were sitting in front of the Phillips' house, trying to sell some Kool-aid in paper cups for five cents. They also had a stack of "funny books" for sale at five cents apiece. Since sales had not been very good, they were relaxed on the grass, under a mimosa tree, sipping a glass of strawberry Kool-Aid and reading the comic books they hadn't seen yet. While deeply immersed in the adventures of Archie and Jughead or Superman or Captain Marvel, they were suddenly surprised by a "Popsicle boy." All Popsicle boys were black and about twelve to fourteen years old. They typically rode a black bicycle attached to a white tin cooler, which was supported by two bicycle wheels in the front. It was like a reverse tricycle. In the cooler were orange, strawberry, grape, and sometimes lemon or lime Popsicles, an ice treat mounted on two sticks. In addition there were Eskimo Pies, chocolate covered ice cream bars on a stick. The white boys eagerly gathered around when the black boy opened the cooler and released the delicious cold smoke of the dry ice inside. Then they inspected his wares, trying to decide which Popsicle they would buy with the few nickels they had earned that day. All of them lusted after the ice cream bar, but at a dime each they were much too expensive. Another attraction of the ice cream bar was that you could be sure the boy hadn't licked it. Todd was convinced that the Popsicle boys took the paper off and licked every one of the Popsicles and then put the paper back on.

"That way he can have a Popsicle and not buy one!" he argued. But that notion was not generally accepted.

"What's your name?" asked Graham, as he tore the paper off of his orange Popsicle.

"I'm Crayton. What's yores?"

"Graham"

"Graham...Cracker! Hee Hee!"

"Huh?"

"Nuthin'"

Graham's eyes crossed as he tried to look at the twin orange ice cylinders while gingerly biting into one of them. He didn't want the cold to hurt his teeth, and he didn't want the ice to suddenly crack and fall off of the stick onto the street. Turning the lovely morsel around in his mouth with his tongue, he moaned with satisfaction, "Ohummm! Don't you ever eat one of these yourself? They're so good on a hot day."

"No! I got to pay the man three cent for every one I sell, so I don't want to bring back no empty cart and no money. He'd take his money out'd my hide!"

"Did ju ever just take one outta the wrapper and take a few licks and put it back?"

"No! I never done such a thing!"

"Okay. But how come my Popsicle tastes like tobacco juice?"

"Huh?"

Looking askance at Crayton while gingerly taking a third

small bite, Graham said, "Have you ever...fooled around with a girl?" Crayton, looking at Todd and Blake lying in the grass enjoying their treats, turned his head and looked sheepishly at Graham,

"The little girl next door come over one day and did'n have no panties on. I took her into the back and we played around some. How 'bout chew?" Graham took the ice treat away from his mouth and looked at the ground self-consciously.

"Yeah, same kinda thing. My little cousin was visitin' from Mississippi... and we wuz hidin' in a closet..."

A sudden clap of thunder saved Graham from further embarrassment and at the same time reminded him that God knows everything, all the time. Immediately after the thunder came a heavy downpour.

Crayton quickly lay the bicycle down in the grass of the Phillips' lawn and joined the three white boys huddled around the trunk of the mimosa tree. The tree offered a fair amount of protection as they scrunched together to avoid drips from the drooping pink blossoms and to conserve body heat. Todd had quickly thrust the comic books under the apple crate they had been using as a table for the Kool-Aid stand. Now he looked at it with dismay, having realized that the spaces between the wooden slats were letting rainwater get in. While he was quickly reviewing ways to protect the comic books from further damage, Mrs. Phillips called out from her front door and told the boys to go get in her garage. Todd quickly ran out, grabbed the comic books and crate and ran to catch up with the other three boys running to the back of the house. While all three panted breathlessly in the musty, dusty dark of the Phillips' garage, wiping rainwater out of their eyes, Blake suddenly cried out,

"The funny books!"

"I got 'em, dummy!"

"That's good!"

"Good thing you and Graham got me around to do your thinkin' for you!"

Graham pushed open the large wooden door of the garage so they could get more light. They sat down on the dirt floor to watch the rain. Blake got up to look for a stick and found a 2X4. He peeled off a large splinter and went back to the doodle bug crater he had found on the garage floor. He stuck the splinter into the hole, wiggled it, and chanted, "Doodle bug, doodle bug, come out, come out. Your house in on fire."

Graham and Crayton continued their conversation, with Todd joining in.

"Whatchew white boys think about Jackie Robinson goin' to the Majors?"

"He ain't goan last," said Todd. "Nig...Coloreds doan know how to take the game serious."

"Well, that mean you white boys ain't never seen the Negro League play. They ain't no picher nowhere better'n Satchel Paige."

"Who's he?" asked Graham.

"He the best picher in baseball. His curve ball start out towud thurd base then come on 'cross the plate. The umpire caint even see his fastball, so he call it on the sound it make when it crack the sound barrier."

Graham and Todd began talking at the same time, Graham about the Yankees and Todd about the Dodgers. Blake suddenly interrupted with

"I'm gittin' hungry!" All three of the other boys consulted their stomachs and realized that they were hungry, too.

"Where do you eat dinner?" asked Graham of Crayton.

"I brung me a ham biscuit and a jug of wahter. It's in the cooler."

"Well, the rain's lettin' up, so I'm goan head for home," said Graham.

"Me, too," said Blake.

Both boys had started out the door when Todd yelled,

"Don't forget our stuff, turds!"

The Flournoys

"Susan, hurry up!" Anna yelled up the staircase. She pressed her hands on her apron to wipe off the flour. "School's out but work is not! Daddy's already eating his breakfast, and I'm putting yours on the table! The biscuits will be hot out of the oven!"

"Mama, I can't find my cute jumper! Is it in the laundry or has Nancy been in my stuff again?!"

"It's not in the laundry! Just wear your new yellow sundress today! I'll look for the jumper later!"

Tall and brown-haired like her father, Susan, sixteen, was a junior at Riverton High and would be keeping her job at the school board office over the summer. She enjoyed the people she worked with downtown. Verifying attendance data for the school district was a boring job. But she was motivated to make money for college, which she would need in only about a year.

Her older siblings, Harold and Maxine, had already graduated from college. Harold was working for the State Department in Washington, D.C. and was "helping to find communists." Maxine had recently graduated from college and married. She and her new husband would start teaching careers in the fall.

"I'm glad Ruthelle's not here today," said Pete as he sipped his black coffee. Pete was seated at the kitchen table, which seemed a bit too small for his lanky frame. "Just before she left to go home yesterday she asked me about borrowing Maxine's wedding dress."

Anna turned her head quickly toward Pete. The hand holding the spatula was suspended over the biscuits she was separating from the baking sheet. She had a perplexed look on her face.

"I wonder why she didn't ask me. After all, I'm the one who made it."

"I dunno. I've been wondering about that, too. Maybe she thought it might be more proper to ask the man of the house about such a matter, since it certainly isn't customary for white people to lend clothes to coloreds. What do you think?"

"Well, she's like a member of the family as you know.

She's the only maid Graham has ever known. The other children love her almost like a mother. We've known her daughter Gaylene since she was...what? Four or five? And Gaylene is almost like a daughter to <u>me</u>. If she were white there'd be no question about it...but I feel uncomfortable about that much familiarity."

"I do, too, but I can't really give you a good reason. I suppose we could lend the dress and hope no one hears about it, but that's not likely. I can just hear the talk now: 'I always knowed that <u>Doctor</u> Flournoy wuz a nigger lover. This here prooooves it!'"

Pete had always tried to avoid controversy, but it always seemed somehow to raise its ugly head. When the national school lunch program had gone into effect the year before, he had made arrangements to have the benefits apply to the black schools as well, perhaps being naïve as to how virulently racist some people could be. Fortunately, he was a native of Alabama and had done his undergraduate studies at the University of Alabama. He hated to think how bad his problems as superintendent would be if he were a "carpetbagger."

"Let's you and me think about this for a while," Pete continued. "And I would also like to involve Susan. She's old enough to discuss the issues, and it would be educational for her. Racial segregation <u>will</u> be ended eventually, and it will be her generation that will pay the price. That young attorney, George Wallace, is making surprisingly progressive statements in his campaign speeches, but I don't hold out much hope for his candidacy."

Anna placed the basket of fresh biscuits on the breakfast room table just as Susan, in her yellow sundress, flowed into the dreary atmosphere like a ray of sunshine. As her father explained the situation to her, her sunny disposition faded while she slowly munched on a biscuit.

Nancy woke up when Susan was leaving the east bedroom they shared. She bounced out of bed happy in the knowledge that the bathroom was free. A single bathroom for the whole family made one resourceful in order to get sufficient bathroom time. Anna would scold the children if one of them yelled, "Give it a lick and a promise!" through the door in an attempt to speed up a brother or sister. Anna was disgusted by the image that evoked. Perhaps they were thinking about dog behavior, she had concluded. Pete would just suppress a giggle and ignore it.

Nancy was a seventh grader at Prentiss Junior High and a little taller and a little heavier than the other girls in her class. "I wonder what Elizabeth is wearing this morning?" Nancy said out loud to herself as she danced in loops on her way to the bathroom. She was thrilled that there would soon be a royal wedding. Great Britain's Princess Elizabeth was engaged to Phillip Mountbatten, Duke of Edinburgh. News of the event was in the paper every day, and the female students at the school had talked about it all spring. It was all "sooo romantic" she had decided. She had bought a Princess and Phillip paper doll book and was in the middle of cutting out and coloring all the figures. She knew she was a little old for paper dolls, but she decided to do it anyway and just not tell her girlfriends. After brushing her teeth she ran back into the bedroom, brushed her dark brown hair, and threw on a skirt, "tennis shoes" and a sleeveless blouse. She then ran down the stairs three at a time, and as she burst into the breakfast room the conversation suddenly died--but she didn't notice.

"What do you girls think about this Kon-Tiki voyage," said Pete, thumping the newspaper next to his plate.

"We talked about it a little in science class," Susan responded. "It sounds scary, but I would just love to be on that raft! Can you even imagine what kinds of fabulous sea creatures they will see?"

"Mrs. Lipton mentioned it one day when we were doing a science lesson," said Nancy as she took her seat. "I would be scared to death on that raft. If a storm didn't destroy the boat and drown you, you'd get eaten by a whale or a shark!"

"I hope you girls understand that the trip is not being taken by Mr. Heyerdahl and his crew to see if they can survive it," said Pete. "The purpose of the voyage is to determine the degree of likelihood that the peoples of the South Sea Islands migrated there from South America. The Kon-Tiki was built using native materials of Peru. Thor Heyerdahl and his crew are attempting to ride the currents and winds for several thousand miles without benefit of modern technology. Of course, they have a radio to call for help in case of an emergency, but they will not use it to help them reach their destination."

"I hope they took plenty of suntan lotion," said Anna, as she took her seat at the table. "It gets awful hot out there in the South Seas. Would that be cheating?"

"Good question. Probably so," said Pete. "My guess is that they are using what they believe was used back then."

"Sounds awfully exciting," said Susan, as she poked at her scrambled eggs.

THE NURSERYMAN AND
THE ARCHITECT

RAYMOND LEWIS WAS A GOOD next-door neighbor to the Flournoys. Neither he nor his wife Ruby showed any overt signs of jealousy for having an ordinary, 1500 square-foot house next door to the aging but still impressive Flournoy manse. The only blemish to their relationship was the fact that Ruby would not allow the neighborhood children inside their house, which baffled Graham especially since their big house was always open to everyone, just about all the time. Anna would occasionally see a strange child at the dinner table when she was serving the food and would just shrug her shoulders, ask the child's name, and get him a plate from the cabinet.

Because she had children of her own—-Todd and his older brother Clark—-Ruby worked hard at maintaining the domestic serenity of her home, which meant her own children were strictly disciplined and no other children were allowed in the house. She had grown up poor on a small farm in south Alabama and was determined to make a better life for herself. She had been fortunate enough to find Raymond, a man with a job during the Depression, and convinced herself she loved him. Ray, also from an impoverished farm family, had a job as the only employee of the only farm supply store in Blalock County, Russell's Feed and Seed, and he was lonely. They had now been married fifteen years.

Brushing her coal-black hair out of her eyes with the back of her hand while packing her husband's lunch, Ruby said,

"Ray, would you bring home some of that beautiful hydrangea Jesse was potting yesterday? I've got a couple of spots in the yard where I think they would do just fine. The Flournoys don't have any hydrangea do they? ...Otherwise I could get a clipping from Mrs. Flournoy. And when you get home tonight I wish you would have a talk with Todd. He stays gone all day with those other boys, and there's no tellin' what they are gettin' into. They're cuttin' through the yard all the time, and spendin' a lot of time on the Flournoy side of the back fence. And you know about the other day when he came home late and wet from Meader's Creek. I don't like not knowin' what my children are up to. At least I know Clark is in summer school in the morning. Mrs. Taylor would call even if he wuz late. But in the afternoon he is almost as bad as Todd. He's on the phone with his friends talkin' about fast cars and planes — -probably fast women too now that he's thirteen. He's thrilled by that breaking the sound barrier business. That whole thing just makes me nervous. Supposin' it's more than the sound barrier that gets broken? I haven't got over the <u>A-bomb</u> yet. "

Throughout this monologue, Raymond sat impassively eating his hard fried egg, crisp bacon, and grits mixed with hot bacon grease. For bread he had slightly burnt toast. He much preferred biscuits, but Ruby had said she didn't have time to make them. He had learned to pretend to be listening and to give a re-assuring grunt every minute or so while thinking about the endless problems of operating both a flower shop and a greenhouse. While wiping his mouth on his cloth napkin and standing up to leave, he broke in to say

"Ruby, I'll bring you some of that gardenia when...

"Hydrangea!"

"...<u>hydrangea</u> when I come home. But I may be a little late. I need to stay after work and have a talk with that Yankee employee I agreed to hire as a favor to Mrs. De Bartelaben at the church. That boy is gettin' to be more and more of a problem. He can't be over twenty-five years old, but he thinks he knows what's best for Alabama. I'm goan tell him that Alabama ain't another New Jersey, and if he thinks it is he better go back to the first one. He's been with us maybe two months and already talkin' about labor unions and racial equality. I'm goan tell him that if he was colored he'd already be at the bottom of the river with a big rock tied to his foot."

With these last pronouncements Raymond took his lunch pail from Ruby, his hat from the pegboard next to the back door and walked into the garage to his brand new, dark blue Chevrolet. He wanted that car to show he was a successful businessman. The car to him was like the house to Ruby. As he drove out of the driveway, it gave him great satisfaction to glance over the hedge at the Flournoy's faded green 1941 Oldsmobile.

The Armistead house was two doors west of the Flournoys. Designed by Nathan, it was small but resembled the big houses, with its upper porch and wooden columns on the tiny front porch. Nathan had made it a tall, skinny house because of the narrowness of the lot – -deep but narrow. But he also wanted a suggestion of the grandeur of the country estates. To the children it was another big house, but to the other adults it should have had only one story. To them it was as artificial and pretentious as the Aldrich house was natural and modest. Even the most status-conscious, insensitive resident of the hill appreciated the tasteful understatement of the Aldrich house. They accorded it nothing but the greatest respect, as they did its sole occupant, Ruth St. John.

In the cool early morning air, Nathan stood on the front porch with his wife Marsha Louise and discussed the day's activities. Blake had already run up to Graham's, and Janie, eleven, was reading *Screen Star* magazine on her unmade bed. She was waiting to be picked up for a day of swimming at Farragut Springs south of the city. Her red, one-piece swimsuit and suntan lotion were wrapped in her beach towel at the foot of the bed. She was thinking about taking a sweater because of how cold she would get swimming in the ice cold spring water. "Maybe I won't go in the water," she said to the studio photograph of Alan Ladd in the magazine.

On the front porch, Nathan shifted his weight. "To answer your question, I don't know what the white folks will think about living next to a Jewish country club, Hon," he said to his wife, who was standing there in a print house dress with her arms crossed over her protruding stomach. The baby was due in about two months. "The developer got this land at a good price," he continued, "and we should be able to squeeze in a dozen houses or so and sell them at a nice profit. Housing is in such demand now that I don't think the buyers are gonna care too much about it. They'll just have to get used to lookin' out their winduhs and seein' rich Jews play golf. I know it's gonna be hard to take for some of them, seein' country club Jews when some of their white friends can't find decent housing.... I just wish you wouldn't always be thinking about the...uh...social consequences of everything we do. Maybe you should be more like Joyce Needham at the office. She thinks it's great that we'll be mixin' Gentiles and Jews. Even though she was born and raised in Riverton, you'd swear sometimes she was from New Yawk City--if it weren't for that thick Southern ac--"

"Joyce Needham is a b--, Nathan!" said Marsha Louise, catching herself at the last second. She had been brought up to believe that ladies never use foul language. Her mother had even added the admonition, "If you can't say something nice about somebody, then don't say anything at all."

"She comes from a well-to-do family and can afford to say what she thinks. I can't. I've got to think about this family and our future, Nathan. Maybe we should love all the Jews and nigras and a-rabs and bring 'em all into our homes and sit 'em down at our tables and wait on 'em. But that just ain't the way things are. I know Rev. Lowndes says that we should love our fellow man, but he also says that the nigras would be uncomfortable trying to live like white folks. We need to love 'em but keep 'em in their place." Waving away a fly trying to land on her nose she continued, "You know I love mama's maid, Flossie, like a mama. She wiped my nose and my fanny from the day I was born and popped me when

I didn't act like a lady. I would do just about anything for her. But askin' her to live like a white person? I would never do that to her."

Nathan was already fidgeting with his car keys, so Marsha gave him a quick kiss on the cheek and gently pushed him off the porch. As he drove out the driveway in his war surplus jeep, He thought about the Trent model blueprints he was working on, a design which offered "elegant living at a modest price."

A Bus Trip to
the Picture Show

The boys were excited about the new picture show downtown at the Arcadia, "Tarzan and the Lost City of Gold." They emptied their piggy banks and counted out eighty-five cents, more than enough for all three. Barefooted but dressed in clean short pants and Tarzan tee shirts, they sat on the front porch steps of Graham's house and watched out for the bus.

"Do y'all think we should build a mawk orange cannon?" said Blake, as he dug into a doodle bug hole with a stick in the dirt next to the steps.

"Nah," said Todd. "The cannon's only good against a fort, and they won't have one. We gotta think of somethin' else."

"Maybe we shouldn't even try to defend our fort!" said

Graham, jumping up and facing the other two boys. "Maybe we could fix up some dummies to look like us up in the tree house, and after they get the cannon set up and shootin' at us we can attack from their flanks!"

Both of the other boys nodded slowly as they considered the merit of Graham's suggestion. After a few more minutes of planning, they began discussing the Tarzan film.

"Ralph Butler saw the show yesterday," said Graham. "He stopped by last night while I was trying to get some lightnin' bugs in a jar. He took a butcher knife from his belt and started throwin' it at a tree. He said Tarzan threw his knife and killed a leopard chargin' at him."

"Don't tell us the story!" yelled Todd and Blake.

"Well, I told him he was gonna get both us in trouble. My mama would be mighty mad if she saw us playin' with a sharp knife and diggin' the bark out of a front yard tree. His mama would be mighty mad if she knew he was playin' with a sharp knife and throwin' her good butcher knife at a tree."

"Did Ralph git invited to fight? Does he have any slingshots yet?" asked Todd. Before Graham could answer, Blake shouted, "There goes the bus!" and all three boys ran across the road to wait in the Robinsons' driveway for the bus to return from the end of the line, which was just a quarter mile down the road.

As the orange and green city bus pulled up to the gravel driveway, the boys saw that the driver was "Popeye." The children called him that because he had extra large forearms. He loved to tease them, and he once held Blake upside down by his ankles to shake the money out of his pockets. Not wanting to have a run-in with him this day, they boarded in quick succession, flung their nickels into the coin receiver, and quickly walked to their seats in the middle of the bus. They would have run but knew better than to give Popeye an excuse to harass them. They had too much to think about.

With the bus underway, Graham, seated next to the window, looked at a metal plate just above his head that he had seen before but hadn't thought about. At the top of the plate was the word "White" and an arrow underneath pointed to the front. Just below was the word "Colored" and an arrow pointed to the rear. For a few seconds he considered what the plate meant before asking the other two boys about it.

In a loud whisper Todd said, "You dummy! That means that the niggers gotta sit in the back of the bus and the whites in the front."

When he said that, Graham glanced at the back. He saw three heavy black women talking, one in her domestic uniform, and a young black man with a pencil mustache staring out the window. Blake had not heard the exchange.

47

He was making truck noises and pretending to shift gears while he studied a poster above his head. It advertised a trucking school.

"I <u>know</u> they gotta sit in the back," said Graham. "I just want to know why."

"Because they stink," Todd whispered loudly, in his typical why-are-you-so-dumb manner.

"Ruthelle don't stink," Graham said. They continued their discussion while Blake got louder and more animated as he drove his imaginary truck. The bus pitched and rolled its way past Trinity College and through some older sections of the city. All of the residential streets were in shadow under a solid canopy of shade trees. But when they passed the First Baptist Church and entered Marshall Boulevard, the main business street, the sunlight suddenly burst upon them.

Popeye turned left on Marshall and made a stop in front of the Bon Marche dress shop. The boys scrambled off the bus from the rear entrance. A half a block west was the Arcadia and its lovely marquee, "Tarzan and the Lost City of Gold."

"Oh, no!" cried Blake, pointing at a group of boys standing in line to get tickets. Todd and Graham saw the problem immediately. Standing in the middle of the line was Murray Austin, a head taller than the other boys. They also recognized Butch Avery, his best friend.

Freckle-faced, with thick, reddish hair, in dress pants,

short sleeve shirt and black Keds, Murray was the only child of a Gentile father and Jewish mother. Having a Jewish mother made him officially Jewish, but he hated to be called a Jew. He avoided the company of boys his age and played with nine- and ten-year olds, who didn't dare call him a Jew. His bar mitzvah the year before had been quite painful for him, despite all the celebration and presents.

"Well, look who's here!" shouted Murray. "If it ain't the River Road Rats! I hear you boys get to fight this year. You ready for a butt whippin'!? Me and Butch are loadin' up his daddy's wheelbarrow with mawk oranges and oilin' the wheels of the cannon. I sure hope you sissies build a better tree house than you did last year!" Murray kept up his relentless taunts until they paid their dime and got inside the cool theater.

At the concession stand in the lobby, Graham paid a nickel for a box of Milk Duds, Blake paid his nickel for a Baby Ruth, and for his nickel Todd got a bag of popcorn. They ran toward the auditorium while shoving each other to be first in. They were quickly brought up short by the teenage usher, who threatened to hit them with his flashlight. Before the feature film, they saw a newsreel about the re-construction of war-torn Europe, the latest chapter of the "Double Bar W Ranch" serial, a Joe McDoakes short subject, and a Bugs Bunny cartoon. After the Tarzan film was over the three boys ran up the block to the bus stop, laughing and jostling each other. Each one wanted to be Tarzan and said the other two could be Cheetah and his sister.

After boarding a bus designated "River Road," Todd and Blake talked about the Tarzan film they had just seen, occasionally acting out a particularly exciting scene. Graham was seated behind them but didn't feel like joining the discussion. Although he wasn't following the conversation, when Blake got out of his seat and stood in the aisle with both arms extended over his head, Graham knew he was re-living the scene when Tarzan dove off of the cliff into the lagoon and wrestled a crocodile swimming toward Boy.

Graham just wanted to stare out the window at the passing scenery and think about why the white people sat in the front and the "colored" in the back. In the Tarzan movie all of the black people were "natives," each with a bundle on his head. One of the blacks wore a fez and carried a whip, and this indicated that he was in charge of the bearers. In one scene, when the safari was traveling a narrow path on the face of a cliff, a bearer lost his balance and fell hundreds of feet to his death, screaming all the way down. The black man in the fez paid no attention to the poor man's death and just yelled at the others to keep moving, and would hit them with his whip if they didn't move fast enough.

The bearers reminded Graham of the black women who

walked through the neighborhood with baskets of fresh pole beans, squash, okra and other popular summer vegetables. These women balanced the baskets on their heads, leaving their hands free. They sang out what they had as they walked from house to house, "Fresh pict po' bee-eens! Collar' gree-eens! Mustud gree-ens!" This would alert the housewife that the vegetable woman would soon be at her back door. Graham's thoughts then turned to a particular woman who sold vegetables in his neighborhood.

I wonder if colored people have a flatter head than white people. I've never seen a white person balance a basket or bundle on their head. I like the veg'table woman. She wears that red and green scarf on her head and that big yellow and purple skirt. She's the only grown person I've seen barefooted – except at the swimmin' pool. When she's carryin' that basket her head is so still. The only thing movin' is her feet. It seems like she just rolls along. She's gotta be strong, too, the way she flips that big ol' basket off her head on the steps like it was nothin'. I'm surprised how rude Ruthelle was to her the last time she came. When Ruthelle came to the back door the veg'table woman said a cheery "Good mornin'" and gave a beautiful white smile. All Ruthelle did was frown and say, "How much yo' coan?!" What is it about colored people who carry stuff on their head? Why is everybody mean to them?

The Rangers Get a New Leader

"AH EE AH EE AH ee ahhhh!" screamed "Mister" Warren, as he swung from one wisteria vine to another, in the Flournoy side yard. His real name was Richard, but his father had called him Mister since he was a toddler, so all the boys called him that too. Mister had also seen the Tarzan movie and wanted to play Tarzan all day, but with the battle drawing near the boys had to concentrate on battle plans.

They had all been shocked and dismayed the night before to learn that none of the older boys would be able to fight. One older boy had to attend summer school unexpectedly, another fell and broke his leg and had gone to stay with an aunt in Montgomery, and two others had landed summer jobs as assistant camp counselors. This meant that Graham, the oldest of the "little boys," would be the leader.

He and the other boys had been in many chinaberry fights but not the fight with the boys from Ramar. He wanted to phone Murray and call off or postpone the battle but was talked out of it by Todd.

Now the whole "army" was gathered in the tree house fretting about the turn of events and making slingshots. In addition to Todd and Blake, Graham invited Ralph, Mister and Lonnie to join the River Road Raiders. Mister ran over from the wisteria vine in the side yard and was trying to rig a rope swing from the tree house to the ground. He half-convinced them that it might come in handy in case of a hasty retreat. Also, Ralph whined about the whipping he got the day before for taking the butcher knife.

"How many men do you think Murray will have?" inquired Lonnie. This would be his first chinaberry battle, since the Ridges had moved to the neighborhood only a few months before. He was a little frightened but didn't want to let on to the others. Of course, the others were scared, too. This year they would be actually fighting. The year before they had been just "runners" and "medics."

"I can be a scout!" said Mister excitedly. I'll tie some ropes from tree to tree and swing out to where I can see 'em comin.' Then when I spy 'em I can swing back and tell you where they are and what they're doin.' They won't be able to see me up in the tree."

Todd and Graham spoke simultaneously, condemning his harebrain plan. Todd continued, "You're gonna have to fight alongside the rest of us. Now if you want to sit up in a tree off from the fort, that might give us some needed crossfire."

"What about Graham's idea of puttin' dummies here in the fort and hidin' out off to the side?" asked Blake.

"I think havin' one man in the fort with the dummies would make it look more real," offered Graham. "Mister can be in that mulberry tree over there, Ralph and Lonnie can be behind the chicken house, and Todd can be hidin' over in the rose garden. The only place they can get the cannon through the hedge from the golf course is through that gap behind Todd's house. That means they will come along the fence, away from all the brush, until they reach the clearing. What we need to do is to help 'em stay along the fence and not find some other way in. If we can direct them so they come to the fort the way we want them to, then we can get 'em in a crossfire. We need to go smooth out the way along the fence and put up brush as blockades everywhere else. That way they'll walk right into our trap!"

Even before Graham finished speaking, Mister scurried off to the mulberry tree and climbed into the lower branches, looking for a place to tie a rope. While looking he ate several of the mulberries and soon had a purple-stained mouth.

"I got an idea!" yelled Ralph. "Art's leavin' for camp tomorrow and I know where he hid some firecrackers!" The boys paused to remember the fireworks display put on the previous New Years by Art, Ralph's older brother. He had gotten one of those big boxes of assorted fireworks for Christmas, including what the boys called cherry bombs, ash cans, zebras, lady fingers (so small they were suitable only for girls), skyrockets, bottle rockets, torpedoes, roman candles, and (also for girls) sparklers.

What Ralph had in mind is what they had seen his older brother and his friends do just after New Year 's Day. They discovered that a zebra encased in a mud ball made an effective hand grenade.

The boys had seen Art and Todd's older brother Clark demonstrate the technique. Art scooped up a handful of mud and molded it into a "grenade." He then stuck a zebra down into the top, leaving only the fuse exposed. Next, he cocked his hand behind his head and Clark struck a match and lit the fuse. When the fuse was burning good, Clark tapped Art on the shoulder and Art threw the grenade high in the air. It exploded just before hitting the ground. To make the second one go off sooner, they lit the fuse closer to the firecracker.

The animated discussion about the grenades continued until they decided that the grenades would make an effective countervailing force against the mock orange cannon, and that Todd and Ralph would form an "artillery team" with an arsenal of mud grenades.

RUTH REMEMBERS ROMANCE

THE ONLY REGULAR VISITORS RUTH had were Germaine the maid, who came twice a week to cook and clean; Mr. Radcliffe, who delivered her groceries every Friday, and Harvey, her "yard man." Pete Flournoy had told her more than once to call him if she needed anything. Once early in the spring she asked him to come over and get a rat snake out of her kitchen, but had not called since. Ruth missed Rachael very much. Without her sister to keep her company, she spent increasingly more time looking out of the windows —- and <u>into</u> herself.

Ruth peered through a sidelight next to the front door and scanned the porch. "I've got to get Harvey to look at that loose board on the front steps. If I stumble on it I could break my neck. Some of the others are getting loose. I probably need a carpenter to rip out the whole thing. No telling how old those stairs are.... Rachael, do you remember the time you ripped your pantaloons on a nail on those stairs? I could see your pink fanny through the rip. Mama and Daddy had company, sitting on the porch. You were sooo embarrassed. Went running around the house and came in the back door. The adults had a nice laugh out of it."

At the memory of the scene Ruth chuckled as she strolled down the hallway and into the kitchen. She stopped at the back door and looked through the glass panels at the peach trees and the chicken house beyond them. "Glad I remembered to have Harvey put some fertilizer on those trees. The fruit looks good. Hope we don't get any worms this year."

Her gaze rose slightly to fall on the old chicken house, which hadn't been used for many years and was now just a haven for copperheads, rat snakes and spiders. She didn't dare go in there. When a breeze came up and the privet bush behind the chicken house began to sway, she was suddenly reminded of the summer when she was twelve, and she was in that thicket with Ray Lee Johnson, who was thirteen. They each grabbed a handful of the tiny blue berries and pushed them into their mouths and began spitting berries at each other at increasingly closer range.

Patooie!

Patooie! Hee Hee!

Pa-tooie!!

Ray Lee! Stop it! You're getting them all in my hair! Mama's gonna be mad!

She recalled how Ray Lee drew close and began picking the berries out of her hair but then very suddenly rose up on tiptoes and kissed her on the mouth. For a second or two they both just stood there looking at each other and blushing. Then the taller Ruth regained her dignity and slapped him across the face.

"Then the strangest thing happened," Ruth said out loud while fingering her pearl necklace. "Instead of looking shocked or crying, he <u>smiled</u>. I can still see his toothy grin as he stood there with his hand pressed against his freckled face. Then he turned and ran as fast as he could down the road."

After a big sigh Ruth continued, "I wish I hadn't been such a lady. I should have grabbed him and kissed him back. I wish I had dragged him deeper into those bushes and...." Ruth would surprise herself with regrets for "missed behaviors" she could now enjoy the guilt of in her old age. Ray Lee never tried to kiss her again.

Thinking about Ray Lee reminded her of the Bobby Langford incident when she was sixteen. She was invited by Roy Duncan to go on a hayride and picnic. Roy was bookish and frail, whereas Bobby was handsome, athletic and charming. Most of the girls had a crush on Bobby but didn't give Roy a second look.

"I wanted so badly to go on that hayride, and when Roy asked me to go I accepted." After clearing her throat, she continued, "I thought he might try to kiss me during the ride. I was certainly feeling romantic enough, sitting high on that deliciously sweet smelling hay in the back of the wagon. I remember that there was no moon, but the sky was clear, and a million stars filled the sky. Whenever the chaperone sitting next to the driver looked distracted, some of the boys would steal a kiss, and the girls' giggling would draw the chaperone back to his duties. I wished I had a reason to giggle, but Roy was too much the gentleman and just sat there looking at the stars. I wish he could have seen the stars in my eyes.

"Later, after we finished our hot dogs, root beer and cookies, we were sitting around the campfire singing songs. I had to use the privy, so I left the circle and went off just beyond the clearing to where the privy was. Then, not wanting to go back to the circle right away, I strolled down to the lake and stood looking at the reflection of the stars in the water.

When I felt an arm around my waist, I gasped and tried to leap forward, but I was held tight. Then I felt a face next to mine and a voice softly saying, 'Relax, Ruth. It's only me.'

It was Bobby. Even though I did not like his rough manner, I was intrigued by his manly presence and his soft, sweet voice. He turned me around and began kissing me along the side of my face. I couldn't help myself. I closed my eyes and went limp in his arms. The next thing I knew he had his right hand cupped under my left breast, gently squeezing and caressing. It was a delicious feeling but also terrifying. I was suddenly overwhelmed by guilt and jerked free. I hit him on the chest as hard as I could and told him things I'm glad I can't remember now. As I stalked back to the clearing, I heard him apologizing and asking if he could call on me.

"I ignored him...Turns out it was the most romantic experience of my life, and I ignored him. I could have become Mrs. Bobby Langford...and I ignored him."

Not wishing to dwell on that memory any longer, Ruth turned away from the window and strolled to her bedroom to take her afternoon nap on her tall, canopied double bed. A couple of years before she had begun using the 3-step mahogany footstool to help her get into the bed. Ruth had decided many years before that the day she could no longer get on her grandmother's bed without using the stool would be the day her old age would begin.

Now, as she lay there, the memory of those romantic encounters so many years before, together with her unsteady walk up the stool's steps, brought home the reality of her advanced age. These thoughts troubled her for several minutes before she finally dozed off.

NED'S BARBER SHOP

PETE FLOURNOY ROUNDED THE CORNER on his way to Ned's Barber Shop, where he stopped by after work on Friday every two or three weeks to get a haircut. His light brown hair was thin and gray at the temples, but it got shaggy on the back of his neck. Ned's was only a couple of blocks from his office building, and he enjoyed taking a brisk walk to the shop. He could also get caught up on local gossip from the men who congregated there. Some, like him, were stopping by after work. Others were retired and just came to enjoy the conversation and waited until a weekday morning to get a haircut.

On this particular Friday it was a little bit hotter than usual. The humidity was close to 100%, so by the time he got to the shop and started to hang up his Panama on the hat rack he noticed the sweatband was dark with sweat.

Looking quickly at his armpits he saw a big half-moon of sweat that had come through not only his shirt but his linen suit coat as well. Heaving a sigh as he hung up the coat and hat, he turned to hear

"Hey, Super!" from Ned's assistant barber, who was busy cutting Josh Doolittle's hair.

"Hey, Bill. Why don't you turn up the heat. I'm freezing," said Pete.

Both men chuckled as Josh said, "Hey, Pete."

In quick succession Pete exchanged greetings with all of the regulars he had been seeing there for years.

"When you gonna fix me up with that kewpie doll teachin' my nephew over at Folsom Elementary?" asked Jim, the youngest member of the group, who was still single and not likely to get married any time soon.

"I have a hard enough time gettin' and holdin' good teachers without inflictin' you on them. She'd be askin' for hazardous duty pay." Both men laughed as Pete took the only chair left.

A few seconds of quiet followed, broken only by the steady hum of the big, oscillating floor fan in a back corner, and the snipping sound of the scissors.

"What do you think, Pete, about Truman mixin' up the races in the arm service?" asked Boyd, the butcher at the A&P.

"Haven't given it much thought, Boyd," which was not true, as he had thought about it a great deal. "Kinda seems like the right thing to do. They fought and died same as we did in the war, so they should have the same privileges it seems to me."

"Don't know about how much fightin' and dyin' they did. When I wuz overseas every colored I ever seen was a cook or a laborer or somethin' like that. Never heard of no coloreds fightin', let alone gettin' killed. I heard they wuz too scared to fight and that's why all of 'em were at the rear someplace," said Boyd.

"Well, I've talked to some colored men right here in Riverton," said Pete. One fought at the Bulge. Another one landed at Omaha Beach."

"Bet he wuz white by the time he got ashore," interjected Phillip. Light laughter rippled through the room.

Pete continued, "Both are teachers over at the colored high school. One of them was an officer. The main reason so many of them were in support positions was because the War Department was under orders to keep the races segregated."

"Seems to me that once you mix up the races in the service, then it's only a matter of time before you'll be mixing them up right here in Riverton," offered Lucian.

"Yeah," Phillip chimed in. "If we keep movin' the line

that separates the races, pretty soon there won't be no line and one day you're goan have a nigger boy standin' at yo front door, callin' on yo daughter. He'll be so black all you'll be able to see is his white teeth. He'll be smilin' so big because he'll be thinkin' about what he's goan do to yo baby girl once he gets her out on some dirt road." A murmur of agreement made its way along the row of chairs.

"If I ever see a buck nigger standin' in front of my door," Phillip continued, "that's goan be one dead nigger." Additional murmurs of assent made their way around the shop.

"I hear talk that Strom Thurmond and some of the other South Carolina boys are thinking about forming their own party for the '48 election," said Beau, one of the retirees, who read two newspapers every day.

"We gotta do sumpin," said Ned, hesitating with his scissors. "If this mixin' keeps up I'm gonna have colored customers and I'll have to learn how to cut that steel wool."

"When you goan learn how to cut <u>white</u> hair, Ned?" asked Jim, who was thumbing through a two-month-old *Field and Stream*. Laughter again rippled through the shop.

"Pete, how long before the schools are goan be mixed together?" asked Lucian.

"Tell you the truth, I don't know...but I'm afraid the schools <u>will</u> be mixed someday."

"Not in my day!" shouted Boyd.

"Mine neither!" shouted Phillip.

"I hear the Klan is holdin' a rally to protest Truman's order," said Josh.

"Shoot, Josh, you didn't hear it. You made the announcement yourself," said Jim, putting down the magazine. Slightly nervous laughter rippled through the shop.

The laughter was nervous because one could never be absolutely sure about the men in Riverton--especially the more racist ones like Phillip. There had been a time in Riverton, as in other parts of the country, that Klan membership had been a requirement for holding public office. By 1947, its excesses had greatly diminished its status with the general population. Even though few blacks were registered to vote, it was risky for a politician to openly admit Klan membership.

"You're a good man, Pete Flournoy," said Boyd, "but if I ever hear of you supportin' the mixin' of the races, I'll vote against you, and get all my friends and family to do the same." A brief, embarrassed silence followed.

"You don't need to worry about Pete," said Ned, as he hesitated before putting hot lather around his customer's ears. "He's an Alabama boy same as us, and he knows that mixin' don't work. He'll do his best to keep the races apart."

Pete squirmed a little in his seat and hoped nobody saw it. He knew that integration would come, and he supported the idea, but he had to be very careful not to disclose his true attitude. He hated having to be a hypocrite, but he didn't know how else to handle this extremely delicate issue. County Superintendent was an elected position, so in order to keep himself in office he had to keep the voters happy. Sure, he could draw himself up to his full height and declare his moral rectitude, but all that would accomplish is to force him to take his wife and young children away from a life they loved and to move far away. He was also a little bit worried about self-righteousness.

Who am I to say that I know what's best for these people? Almost all of them are kind and decent, even though they are racists. One of the most Christian women I've ever known, Lisa Bumgartner at church, is also one of the worst racists I've ever known. She is very loving to the coloreds as long as they stay in their place. She would never condone harming any colored person, but she does speak out strongly against race mixing of any kind.

With these thoughts running through his head, Pete picked up a month-old Argosy and pretended to read it so that the men would direct their attention to other matters. After a few seconds of pretending great interest in the page before him, he heard Julian say to no one in particular, "What about that boy Jackie Robinson? You think he can make it in the Majors?"

IRONING OUT THEIR DIFFERENCES

ONE AFTERNOON WHEN GRAHAM CAME home from a strategy session with the Raiders, he found Ruthelle ironing on the back porch. She was humming "Nearer My God to Thee" while expertly pressing one of Pete's dress shirts. She picked up a Royal Crown Cola bottle half full of water and, covering half of the mouth with her thumb, sprinkled another section of the shirt as Graham came through the back door.

"Ruthelle, is Mama home yet?"

"No, chile, she probly won't be back for another hour or so," she said without looking up. "What you needin' that wore-out woman for?"

Ignoring the tease, Graham replied, "Oh, nothin'. I just wondered, that's all," as he sat down on top of the firewood box next to the wall.

"You ready for school to start back?"

"No! I got too much to do. I don't even want to <u>think</u> about school!"

Ruthelle continued with her humming and ironing as she thought about his remark. "What does a ten-year-old boy have to think about on a fine day like today?"

Graham hesitated before answering, as he was not sure he should talk about his troubles with a colored person. "Oh, me and Todd and Blake got a...contest we've entered, and we want to win."

"What kind of contest?"

"It's a...shootin' match. We've been practicin' a lot."

"Well, that's exactly what you got to do to win a contest. Practice. Keep practicin' 'til you're as good as you can be. Then if you don't win it won't be because you didn't try. You gotta believe in yourself, too!" Ruthelle said while bearing down on the iron, its tip darting between the buttons of the shirt.

"Graham Bishop, you're a smart boy and can <u>do</u>. I've seen you do. You gotta just tell yourself that you're goan win that shootin' match. Those other boys got two arms, two legs, one head, same as you. So I aks you, what they got that you don't?

"You need to start lookin' in yo room for a spot to put yo trophy – -or whatever they givin' as a prize. If you look at challenges that way, you got the job half done. If you don't win, it just wasn't meant to be. The Good Lord has other plans for you besides winnin' a shootin' match.

"I remember when my baby brother Maurice wanted to play basketball for his high school team. He was a good player but not great. And "good" wasn't good enough for him. He didn't want to be warmin' a bench. In his last year of junior high he practiced every chance he got. Daddy had him workin' after school at the salvage yard, so he didn't have much time to practice. But he worked hard and made that team. He was their best player." She finished the shirt, put it on a hanger, and hung it on a hook on the back of the door.

"Ruthelle, why don't colored children go to school with white children?"

Stalling for time, she fussed with the next white shirt before answering. "Chile, you're too young to be worryin' 'bout such as that. How come you're loadin' that weight on yo back?"

As soon as she said that she regretted it. She didn't want to appear dissatisfied, even to a family as tolerant as the Flournoys. "Graham, the colored and the whites have different ways of livin'. And keepin' separated is the best way for both of them to live."

"But you and Gaylene aren't different."

71

"Well, in some ways we <u>are</u> different. And that's all you need to know. Now you go get washed up and I'll have you a san-wich before you can say 'Jack Robinson.'"

"Jack Rob-in-son," Graham intoned as he ambled into the kitchen.

Motorcycle Madness

TODD ENJOYED READING HIS BROTHER'S motorcycle magazines. Like Clark, Todd was fascinated with the idea of traveling around a track at 70-80 miles per hour, putting your foot down in the dirt to keep from tipping over in a tight turn. That looked very manly to him. Sitting on his brother's bed, he studied intently the pictures of BMWs, Indians, Triumphs and Harleys screaming along at a 45 degree angle to the dirt track, the racer's steel-tipped boot bouncing off the track to keep from falling over.

Braaap! Todd pedaled his hand-me-down bicycle as fast as he could up his driveway and down Graham's, making as much noise as possible. He had attached the King of Diamonds playing card to the frame with a clothespin. The card protruded into the spokes and crudely simulated the sound of a motorcycle engine.

"Hey, Graham! How you like my motor?" Todd yelled as he slid in the gravel in front of the Flournoy front porch. The spray of gravel from his rear tire flew up on the porch and pelted Graham, who raised his arm to protect his face.

"Watch out, turd! Mama's goan be mad if she sees gravel all over the porch! What motor?"

"<u>This</u> motor!" Todd responded, pointing at the playing card.

"It looks just like the King of Diamonds to me," Graham teased.

"You heard it when I rode in! That was a motor! Clark showed me how to rig it."

"Well, I found out something more fun than riding around with a card stuck in my spokes"

"Yeah? What?"

"Yesterday I was ridin' down Farragut Springs Road with a boy who was in my class last year. We wuz goin' along at a pretty good speed, when all of a sudden he cuts his bike to the right and hits a little hill and goes sailin' off into the woods like he was in a jet plane! I stopped and came back to see if he was hurt and he came ridin' out of the woods grinnin'. He <u>planned</u> to make that jump. Some boys in a neighborhood over there had cleared a track from the road, over the hill and down into the woods. He took me back up the road and told me to follow him. He hit the hill first and went flyin'. Then I hit it and couldn't believe how far I flew through the air! We musta spent the next hour just ridin' up the road and back down to the jumpin' hill. You wanna go try it?" Todd nodded his head then said, "What about Blake?"

"He told me had to go see the eye doctor with his mama. He may have to get glasses. Sure hope he don't. We need all the good eyes we can get for shootin' the Renegades."

Todd nodded again and the two boys rode off alongside River Road until they could cut through a few lots to get to Farragut Springs Road, then south to where the "jumpin' hill" was. They spent the next half-hour jumping until Graham said he had to get home. Todd's jumps had been especially dramatic because of the high-pitched *braaaping* from his front spokes as he raced into the hill.

While they slowly rode back home, Todd, in an unusually pensive mood, broke the silence.

"Graham, you know what I'd like to do someday? I'd like to ride a motorcycle around a track and have hills to jump along the track. That would be sooo much fun! You'd get that motor up around sixty miles an hour and hit a hill and just fly over the track! You'd spend so much time in the air you'd have to have a pilot's license!" Both boys chuckled as they continued their ride back to River Road.

Within thirty minutes of returning home Todd had

contacted all of the Raiders and told them about the jumping hill. With the exception of Graham, who had to go shopping with his mother, all of the Raiders met at Todd's on their bikes. Even Blake was there, feeling especially good since the doctor had told him he didn't need glasses — -yet. Each had brought a tool, carrying it across the handlebars. Two brought spades, one brought an axe, and one brought a swing blade. They sat in a circle on the Lewis's front lawn and discussed jumping and motorcycle noises. Todd went in his house and came out with the King of Clubs, the King of Spades, the King of Hearts and, for Mister, a Joker. He had decided that Graham would get the other Joker. What Todd forgot in his calculations was to ask his mother if he could take cards from the deck. He got into big trouble the next time his parents played gin rummy. While in the house he also pilfered four clothespins.

Two minutes later all five boys and their tools were braaaping alongside River Road toward Meader's Creek where Ralph said there was a hill. If that were a good jumping hill, it would be a lot closer than the one on Farragut Springs Road. Just past the east end of Aldrich was a dirt road that went north through a woodlot and eventually bordered pastureland. Just a short way down the road was indeed a small hill. They stopped and inspected it. Since Todd was the only one with experience jumping, the other boys offered no opinion. Todd inspected the ease of entry into the roadside brush and the grade of the launch side then ordered everybody to dismount and go to work clearing away brush, saplings and grass in the approach path. Those with shovels could also move around dirt as needed.

Within twenty minutes the path in front of and in back of the hill was reasonably clear and level, so Todd showed them how to do it. He rode back up the road for a couple of hundred feet, turned and started back. *Braaap!* The noise from the King of Diamonds grew increasingly shrill as he picked up speed, negotiated the switch from road to path, then rose up from his bicycle seat before hitting the up slope of the hill. The bike flew up into the air and he sailed farther than he had on any of his jumps on the other hill.

The other boys watched, eyes big and mouths open, as he disappeared into the trees. They ran over to the hill for a better view, saw him hit a pine sapling and cry out in pain. They ran into the woods along the landing path to where Todd was bouncing and limping. His bike lay off to the side, handlebars severely crooked.

"What happened?" cried Blake.

"I got a flat tire, dummy!" Todd shot back sarcastically, still limping and bouncing. "Whadaya think happened!? I hit a tree!"

Todd had suffered several abrasions on his legs, but

otherwise was unhurt. He knew he had been showing off and had hit the hill too fast, but he wasn't about to admit his mistake.

"That tree jumped out in front of me!" he joked, then smiled.

The boys helped Todd get his bike out of the woods and then Todd straightened out his handlebars by straddling the fenderless front tire and holding it in place while twisting the handlebars back into position. Without having to be told, all five boys understood from Todd's accident that excessive speed can cause the rider to miss the rather narrow landing path.

For the next hour the boys took turns jumping the hill and discussing ways to widen the landing area so they could travel higher and longer. The main problem they decided was getting rid of the stumps of the pine saplings they would have to remove.

Thoroughly exhilarated and exhausted by the afternoon's discoveries and activities, the boys headed for home, brapping all the way.

They looked forward to drinking a tall glass of ice water from the family bottle in the refrigerator and lying down to rest under a shade tree or on a front porch swing. Sometimes they didn't bother getting a glass and drank directly from the family bottle. But getting caught drinking from the bottle meant getting in trouble.

Todd made the same plans but also added swabbing iodine on his leg abrasions. He didn't want his mother to do it because he didn't want her to know about the injury. Her lecture would make his leg hurt even more. Later, as he made his way to the kitchen for some ice water, he hoped his mother wouldn't notice the five, large, red iodine patches on his bare legs.

DEMONS OF DOUBT

DESPITE HIS EFFORTS TO BE positive and upbeat in his strategy sessions with the Raiders, Graham, being only ten, was very insecure about going up against a captain who was fourteen and had won the battle the year before. Suppose they brought more soldiers than they did last year? What if they find out ahead of time that Graham is the oldest Raider fighting? What if Murray's mock orange cannon is more deadly than it was last year? How could he stand the humiliation of losing and being made a P.O.W.?

It was summer. School was out. He should be free from all worries, but he was not only worried during his waking hours but at night as well. When he played with the other children he pretended not to be worried but he was. He had hoped he could lose himself in a baseball game or a trip to the swimming pool, but he couldn't dispel his worries entirely. He cracked open the door of his father's home office.

"Daddy, can I come in?"

"Sure. What's the problem?" Pete Flournoy had got into the bad habit of assuming that anyone who came to his office door came with a problem. As soon as he said "problem" to Graham, he realized how entrenched the habit had become and regretted saying it. He then tried to compensate by setting down his pen, looking up, and smiling at his son who, with a furrowed brow, walked slowly toward his desk.

"Daddy, I want to talk to you about something man to man. What I mean is...Mama can't know about it."

"Well..."Pete hesitated momentarily to review quickly the topics he felt he could discuss with their children without involving Anna. "I guess so," he answered lamely.

"Mama would put a stop to it, and that would make my life even worse." Pete was now beginning to worry himself and to doubt agreeing to the man to man arrangement.

"Tell me what's bothering you, son."

"Did you know that we have a chinaberry battle with the Ramar Renegades every year?"

"No. Who's 'we'?"

"Me and Todd and Blake and Ralph and Mister and Lonnie--but this will be our first year to fight. Last year, Clark and Richie and the other big boys were in the battle.

81

This year none of the big boys can fight, so it's up to us little boys to represent the Raiders. Last year we were medics and runners and such, so we know a lot about the battle, but we've never actually fought. We know how to fight each other, but the leader of the other army is fourteen..." Graham started to mention the mock orange cannon but quickly caught himself. He was old enough and smart enough to know how dangerous the cannon was and didn't want any adult to know about it. "And his army are good fighters. Last year they beat us."

"Why don't you just cancel the battle this year since none of the older boys can participate?"

"I thought about that, but Clark told me and Todd that we could fight this year, and we want to...uh...keep the honor of the Raiders. If we chicken out the big boys probly won't let us fight next year." Pete momentarily reflected on how regrettable it is that this child should have such weighty problems but then reminded himself how fortunate he is not to have worse problems.

"What have you done so far, about the problem?"

"I wanted to cancel when I found out we would have to fight by ourselves, but Todd talked me out of it. Then me and Todd and Blake made some good slingshots and planned some strategy. Then us and Ralph and the others did some planning. But I'm still afraid we're not ready."

"Tell me exactly what your plans are so far," Pete said as he reared back in his chair and put his hands behind his head. Graham strolled over and sat down in the guest chair.

Graham detailed how they had cleared a path so the Renegades could easily get to the tree house—-without mentioning the cannon. Pete smiled at the ingenuity of that tactic. He told his father about the placement of the Raiders in and around the tree house. Finally, reluctantly, he told him about the firecracker grenades and was relieved that his father was not bothered by them.

"Well, son, I think you have made some very worthwhile plans. You've used your brains to make up for what you lack in size or experience. Do the Renegades know they will be fighting younger soldiers?"

"No, I don't think so."

"Don't let them know. Keep yourselves hidden as best you can and make them think they're fighting older boys. Being dispersed out from the tree house can make your army appear larger than it is. To a great extent warfare is psychological. That is, you have to make the enemy think he is in greater danger than he really is. So you should do everything you can to make the Renegades think you are stronger than you really are. And the <u>opposite</u> of that can also work. Your slingshot battle reminds me of David and Goliath. Tell me what you know about the story."

83

"David killed Goliath with a slingshot."

"That's right," Pete said, tapping his pen on the desk, feeling his teacher persona rise within him. "Now there are two lessons I want you to get from that story. One is that slingshots can be very dangerous. Nobody ever shoots rocks do they?"

"No, we only shoot chinaberries — -with the slingshots."

"Good. The second lesson is that even though he was much smaller and had no armor and had a much smaller weapon, David was able to win the fight. Why was he able to win when the odds were so heavily against him?"

Graham considered the question for a few seconds then replied, "Because he used his head."

"That's right. How did he use it?"

"He made Goliath think that beating him would be so easy that he didn't have to be careful."

"Exactly. Goliath got overconfident. He was the mightiest soldier among the Philistines. He had defeated many valiant, well-armed men and was greatly feared. When he saw that the Hebrews had put a mere boy with a slingshot up against him in single combat, he threw back his head and roared with laughter. His laughter caused him to drop his guard. When he threw back his head to laugh, he unintentionally lowered his sword and shield. "Now David had known for some time that Goliath was to be his opponent and had spent a lot of time planning what he would do. Just as you are planning now. He decided that he could use his smallness to his advantage. He would make himself look even weaker than he was by appearing to be scared to death when he came out. He would be stoop-shouldered and shaking, dressed only in his sheepskin and sandals. He would hold his slingshot in such a way that it looked like he didn't know how to use it.

Goliath had no need for plans because he was so big and strong. Even against his strongest opponents he overwhelmed them with his size and strength. Instead of size and strength, David had brains—-which, by the way, always win in the long run. He knew the history of Goliath's one-sided battles, and his brainless, brutish approach to fighting. He knew that if Goliath took him seriously as an opponent the others would laugh at him, so David calculated that Goliath would have to ridicule him before killing him. And that just might give him an opportunity to catch him off guard. So tell me what happened when Goliath lowered his sword and shield."

"David took a stone from his sheepskin. It was sharp. He put it in the sling and swung the sling around his head three times and let it go. The rock hit Goliath in the forehead and punctured his brain. He fell down dead."

"That's right. Goliath got careless, as David predicted, so

the little boy was able to defeat the big man. Now what else was necessary for David to win?"

Graham pondered the question for several seconds, pulling at his left ear all the while. "He had to make a good shot. He only had one shot, and it had to be a good one."

"Very good. So what's that mean for the Raiders?"

"We've got to practice. We've got to be better shots than they are."

"Exactly! You've got plenty of brains, Graham, and it looks like you're using them. I bet that leader of the Renegades-- what's his name?"

"Murray"

"I'll bet Murray's a lot like Goliath--overconfident and careless. You can beat his brawn with your brains, and skill."

His morale now bolstered, Graham smiled at his father, "Thanks, Daddy. I feel a lot better. I'll get the Raiders together tomorrow and we'll practice all day." He got up out of the chair and walked out of the office.

Pete stopped tapping his pen and gave a sigh of regret that he was no longer ten years old. He then took the thick, year-end school system report out of his briefcase and laid it on his desk.

THE WATERMELON CAPER

BETWEEN LATE MAY AND NOVEMBER, activities around Riverton slowed to the sluggish pace typical of cities and towns in the Deep South. Even though it was not quite summer in the northern latitudes, it was already deep summer in Alabama. In the ninety-degree-plus temperatures, with often near one hundred percent humidity, half of one's energy each day was expended trying to stay cool. Air conditioning was available only in the department stores and movie theaters, so shopping or going to the "picture show" became exceedingly attractive. Everywhere else Southerners depended on electric fans. Each home was equipped with one or more oscillating fans, either a tabletop model or a large floor model. Even better was an attic fan. If you were lucky enough to have an attic fan, you could turn it on and just open any window to get a breeze.

In Chicago, an employee might scheme to get out of work to go to a Cubs game, but in Riverton he would devise a plot to go see a movie--any movie, or go sit under a shade tree and do some cane pole fishing. He could also daydream about Christmas as a way to keep cool. A popular summertime department store sale was "Christmas in July." Another common daydream on a hot summer day was about eating a slice of cold watermelon. There was nothing more satisfying to Rivertonians on such a day than eating cold watermelon.

One particularly hot and humid day, Todd, Graham and Blake were thinking about watermelon and trying to figure out how to get one.

"Boy, I can just taste that juice squirtin' outta my mouth and runnin' down my chin," said Blake, his eyes closed to savor the thought.

"I can feel that cold, red pulp makin' my teeth hurt just a little bit as I bite down slowly an' all that sweet juice fillin' my mouth," said Todd, also with his eyes closed. The boys were having their description contest while sitting cross-legged on the cool floor of the Flournoy front porch.

Graham was not interested in joining the contest because he was still worried about the upcoming battle. He languidly remarked, "My brother told me that when he wuz our age him and his friends used to get watermelons off a delivery truck. He said they would go over to the Farmer's Market early in the mornin' where the truck would be unloadin.' They knew that just as soon as the driver pulled in he wuz ready for a cup of coffee before unloadin'. So while the driver was havin' his coffee, one of the boys would crawl up into the truck and toss down one or two melons to the other boys."

"The Farmer's Market is on the other side of town," groused Todd, as he casually bounced the rubber ball they were using in their jacks game.

"Yeah, but I've been thinkin'. A lot of those trucks come right down the highway here," said Graham, waving his hand in the direction of the road in front of the house. "What if we hide out next to the red light and get one off while the truck is stopped?" Blake and Todd thought about his question for a moment before Blake asked,

"What if the truck starts up before we can get back off?"

"I thought about that. At first I thought maybe jumpin' off would be okay, but then I thought maybe not. Somebody could get killed jumpin' off a movin' truck. Then I thought about the next red light. When he stops for that one we could jump off then."

"Why are you and Blake sayin' 'we'?" interjected Todd. We all can't be up in the truck. Who's gonna catch the watermelons? And another thing. Do y'all have any idea how heavy a watermelon is, especially one comin' at you from the top of a truck? I can just picture Blake gettin' squashed by a watermelon. He'd look like a busted watermelon himself. I can also see in my picture of this cars behind the truck which are also waitin' for the light to change. Whadda we do about them? Wave friendly like?"

"Another thing that worries me," offered Blake, "is that second red light business. What if the truck catches all green lights between here and Montgomery?"

"Well, at least you'd have plenty to eat along the way," said Graham with a chuckle.

This debate continued for several more minutes while they sipped some grape Kool-Aid Anna brought them, along with two vanilla wafers each. By the time they finished the snack and wiped their mouths with the backs of their hands, they had decided on the following plan. They would go over to Trinity College, where the highway (now just called River Road) passed next to the campus and had four traffic lights in half a mile. They reasoned that if they got the melons at the first red light they were bound to get another red light before the truck cleared the last of the four.

The problem of the weight would be handled by having Todd, the strongest, get up into the truck and throw down one melon, two if there is time, to Graham and Blake, who would catch them together. As for the cars behind, they decided that the early morning trucks would be best since it would be unlikely any cars would be out so early.

At 5:00 a.m. the next morning Graham woke up automatically, and since he had only to slip on his short pants with the elastic waistband to get ready, he was standing under Todd's bedroom window thirty seconds later, scratching on the screen.

"Todd? You 'wake?" he whispered.

"Huh? Yeah."

"Meet me at Blake's"

"Yeah. Okay."

When Graham arrived at the Armistead house, Blake was standing at the entrance to the driveway throwing gravel at a sign across the road. The sign showed a curve ahead. The challenge of hitting the sign was compounded by the difficulty of seeing it in the dim early morning light. Graham joined in the sport, heedless of the loud clang of the occasional hit. Soon Todd joined them, and the three boys were off on their adventure, discussing the best way to cool a watermelon.

When they got to the intersection of River Road and Aldrich Road, the site of the first traffic light, they looked for some place to hide next to where the truck would stop for the light and settled on lying in the drainage ditch next to the road. Every minute or so Graham would rise up a little and look up the hill to see what was coming. Three cars and one pickup truck passed, but only one had to stop for the light. Then they saw what looked like a produce truck round the corner. But it went right through on a green light. As it passed, all three rose up to see what the load was and groaned when they saw watermelons under a tarpaulin. Three more cars and two more produce trucks hauling vegetables came by, with three of them stopping for the light.

After thirty minutes the sun was getting high, so the boys were beginning to get hot. Adding to their miseries were the chiggers in the ditch grass, which soon had them scratching all over. Forty minutes into their great adventure and they were sweating, scratching, and getting dizzy from the exhaust fumes of idling cars and trucks which had stopped for the red light.

Just when they thought they couldn't take any more of their fun, Graham saw a produce truck with a tarpaulin round the corner.

"Git down! I think this is the one!"

"Git down? I don't think I can get up," moaned Blake.

"Shudup!" yelled Todd.

When the truck got within a couple of hundred feet of the intersection, and the boys were afraid it would make the green light, the signal turned yellow, the truck slowed, then red, and the truck came to a squeaking stop. Graham quickly noted with delight that no car was coming from behind, so he signaled frantically with his hand for Todd to jump aboard, which he did, in a flash. He pulled back the corner of the tarpaulin and quickly thumped two or three melons to find a ripe one, then grabbed it firmly with his hands. Graham and Blake stood next to the truck with their hands stretched upward, waiting for the toss.

While this was going on, the burly driver of the truck saw Todd through his rearview mirror, got out of the cab, walked down the driver's side of the truck bed, and stood looking up at Todd heaving the large melon up to his chest.

"Hey, boy!!! Whatchew doin' up there? Git down and come here!" Todd was so startled that he dropped the melon and leaped over the heads of the other two boys, landing in the tall grass next to the ditch. With no loss of momentum he was running up the highway with the truck driver chasing after him. Graham and Blake were equally startled and ran as fast as they could up Aldrich Road.

They stopped a hundred yards away and looked back to see the driver walking back to his truck. Just as he got back in the cab a car pulled in behind him and the driver started blowing his horn, but before the truck could move the light changed to red. Then the man in the car got out and hurriedly walked up to the cab of the truck but returned even faster and got back in his car.

The boys were enjoying the mini-drama at the intersection but realized they had better go find Todd. They continued up Aldrich Road until they could find a good lot to cut through to Thurman Road, where they could easily get to Ruth St. John 's back field and then to Graham's house. When they got there, Todd was waiting on the front steps, holding his head with one hand and scratching the chigger bites in his crotch with the other. When he saw Graham, he shouted, "Got any more great ideas, dummy?!"

Rocking and Reminiscing

Early June in Alabama is still fairly cool in the evening, so soon after the sun set beyond the tree line behind the Henrys' back yard, Ruth liked to have a cup of tea on her front porch. In addition to a swing at one end of the porch, she had a capacious oak and wicker chair in front of the parlor windows. On this particular evening, after placing her cup and saucer on the small side table next to the chair, she paused to consider how old the chair was. It had been re-woven a couple of times that she could recall, so she concluded that she and it were about the same age, which made the evening interlude all the more satisfying, to spend it with an old friend. She slowly turned and sat just as the sun disappeared below the horizon. As she gazed at the pink and orange skyline, she contentedly sipped her tea and thought back over her life.

"Rachael, do you remember when the Flournoy house was built?" darting her eyes to the left to look at it. "I can just barely remember seeing them tear down the cotton gin and put up those huge posts at the corners. Reverend Baxter and his family moved in maybe a year later. I did so enjoy visiting the Baxters. I just loved those teacakes Mrs. Baxter would serve us in the tea parties she had for us and Katherine. I remember being jealous of Katherine for having a mother who could make such cakes.

"I never cared much for that next family, the ...oh, what were their names? They spent all their time working in the yard and just when they got it looking beautiful Mr. What's–his-name up and dies. I guess maybe I can't remember their names because I've tried to forget that horrible night when those men on horseback caught that colored man hiding in their back yard. The prancing, froth-sweaty, restless horses, the torchlight, the shadows, the shouting...and then they rode off in a gallop with that colored man tied to the extra horse they brought along. If you remember, Mama and Daddy tried to shield us from all that, but we saw enough. It was horrible...horrible.

"But enough of that!"

After taking another sip of her tea, Ruth became aware of the crickets, katydids and tree frogs tuning up for the evening's serenade.

"I'll never forget the night when I was what? Seventeen? I was sitting on the porch swing with John Marsh. What a nice, strong name. What a nice young man! I remember that you were jealous. His hair was neatly parted in the middle, and he was wearing some nice pomade. He was wearing a clean, starched collar. He was looking at me seriously with those beautiful blue eyes, and he was saying some nice things to me, but when the frogs and insects started up he had to speak louder and then louder to be heard. Hee! Hee! Even in the dim light of the lantern I could see him blushing.

"That's the only time I remember you inside and me out on the porch with a suitor. Seems like the rest of the times it was me peeking through the curtains at you on the porch. There was that one time when I was shocked at what I saw and almost went to tell Mama...I always hated to admit it, but you <u>were</u> the pretty one. I was too gangly and pushy to find a man, but you <u>could</u> have, and I never understood why you never did."

Ruth luxuriated in the increasingly cooler evening air, enjoying the gardenia flowers whose scent wafted across the highway from Mrs. Henry's yard. She didn't have any bushes of her own because up close their scent was too strong.

What Ruth never found out from her "baby" sister was that Rachael was so close to her that she didn't want to leave her alone, having decided that her older sister was destined to be an "old maid." There had been a time just before their grandmother, Dancer, died when Rachael was seriously involved with Nate Richards, but the thought of moving with him to Chicago away from her family was just too much. Even when young, she could picture her older sister all alone in the big house — -which could be quite empty and cold with no people around. Ruth had always watched out for her, and she liked it that way.

As the sunset turned pale blue and gray in the fading light, Ruth recalled the years when Granny Dancer had been sick, then twenty years later when her mother Charlotte had been sick.

"Granny was such a brave soul. I can still see her propped up in that big feather bed wasting away with consumption, but she never complained, and wouldn't accept any help until she was absolutely helpless. I see her reading her bible by the light of the bedside lantern. Then when she could no longer sit up and her eyesight was failing I would read her bible to her.

"She especially liked the epistles of Paul. She once said to me that everyone should be knocked to the ground on the road to Damascus so they could be converted instantly. I never figured out what she meant by that.

"Then there was Aunt Beverly. It must have broken Granny's heart for one of her daughters to go away forever.

I was a young woman when Granny died, and I remember thinking that if this is what marriage is all about, then I don't want any of it. But, you know, Rachael, I don't think it was fair to Mama for both of us not to marry. Remember how she used to quiz us about young men? Remember what she said about a house without children being hollow? When everybody thought you were going to marry that Nate Richards, Mama went out and bought you that trousseau. It's still in the attic. She kept hoping one of us would use it. Poor Mama. Lost her daddy in the War, then her sister went away forever. And her stubborn, selfish daughters refused to get married and give her grandchildren.

"I wasn't as popular with the boys as you were, with your pert little figure. But I had my chances." Ruth broke out in a big smile and rattled her cup in her saucer as she recalled the five men in her life who had taken an interest in her romantically. None of them, however, had ever proposed to her. She only imagined they had, or would have.

"Do you remember Mr. Ferris, the science teacher at Flo Hennessy? He was so handsome. Every girl in the college had a crush on him. I had an awful hard time concentrating in his class. I will never forget the day Sybil Morris and I sneaked into his classroom. I picked up the human skull he had on his desk and did my best Hamlet interpretation. I lifted the skull over my head with one hand, like this, and emoted, 'Alas, poor Yorick. I knew him well!' I think he must have been looking at us through the door window because it was just as I uttered 'well' that he suddenly walked in, laughing, and said, 'Miss St. John, come Friday I hope you will know your cranial and facial anatomy as well as you know your Shakespeare.' I was terribly embarrassed, and Sybil couldn't stop giggling."

The sky now having become charcoal gray, Ruth listened to the night sounds a little while longer then slowly rose from her rocker, picked up her empty cup and saucer, and went back into the house.

The Renegades Prepare for Battle

"Okay, snot jar, where'd you put my slingshot?" asked Murray.

"I ain't seen your slingshot, Murray," replied Butch.

Murray was worried about a favorite weapon he had put together with great care, having rounded up the very best of materials and carefully constructed it. He was afraid that Butch or one of the other boys would steal it, but that seemed unlikely since he knew exactly how it looked, and he had even burned his initials into the leather pouch with the electric "wand" from his wood burning kit. "M.A." was seared into the back of the pouch, and the grooves of the burn gave a little extra traction for the thumb and forefinger when he drew back to fire.

"Well, you better not have it. That's the sweetest 'shot I

ever made." Having decided that he probably left it in his other jeans, which he had changed out of because they were wet, Murray got back to the job of oiling up the mock orange cannon. The oiling involved squirting the thin oil onto the axles and wheels they had taken from the child's wagon and coating the rusted areas of the fan frame. They considered changing out the inner tube for a newer, bigger, stronger tube and calling the new weapon The Howitzer. But they decided it would be too much trouble and take too many hours of their summer vacation, which was short enough as it was.

Butch took one of his dad's discarded undershirts soaked in oil and began to rub a large rust spot on the fan frame, and the longer he talked the more vigorously he rubbed. "I sure hope I don't get Ol' Worm Face next year," groused Butch. "She'll make you stand in the corner when the last bell rings and listen to the boys whoopin' and hollerin' out in the playground. Makes you stand there for a couple of hours, and if you say even one word she adds an hour."

Miss Priscilla Andrews was in her tenth year at Broad Street Elementary, one of two teachers who taught fifth grade. Butch would be in fifth grade the following September and couldn't help occasionally looking ahead to the start of school, especially when occupied doing something with his hands. Priscilla had got her "Worm Face" nickname because of the drastic effects of acne she had suffered as a teenager. The welts were rope-like and angry red, taking on a pink appearance when covered with face powder. The boys had decided that they looked like Red Wigglers.

Her dermatologist had told her about some dermal abrasion techniques that showed promise but were still experimental in nature, so she pretty much had decided to live with the problem.

Priscilla was aware that the boys called her this behind her back. It pained her, but she was professional enough to know that boys are naturally crude and frank. The insult probably did not reflect the individual boy's attitude. It was just something he said in order to be accepted. She sometimes wondered why it was that boys gravitated to the dangerous and vulgar in order to gain acceptance. Why couldn't acceptance, she mused, require getting a library card?

Priscilla knew for sure that some of the boys liked her very much because they would stop by her duplex apartment on a Saturday afternoon to talk. Of course the visit, she knew, was almost certainly kept secret from the other boys. She had decided that probably the worst thing that could happen to the boy would be to get identified as a teacher's pet of Worm Face. This prompted her not to mention the visit to her colleagues for fear one of them might accidentally "spill the beans."

"Sure wish Ol' Worm Face wuz here right now," said Butch, admiring his work on the frame. "I'd sure like to get some wigglers and go fishin'. All this work is makin' me hot and tired."

As he said this, Sam Dougherty and Carl Cristofino, both eleven, walked into Murray's back yard and over to the garage where the "cannon" was being serviced. The garage was a white frame building to the right and rear of the property, with a gravel driveway leading up to it from the street. The gravel hadn't been replenished in several years, so there was only occasional evidence of it among the grass and weeds growing there. After Frank took the car out to go to work that morning, Murray pulled the contraption from the back of the garage to the front where there was more light.

"Why y'all workin' so hard this mornin'? Let's go swimmin' out at the Forresters'," said Sam.

Uninvited Swimming Pool Guests

BOB FORRESTER WAS A WEALTHY architect in Riverton who owned a country estate out on Duggan's Gap Road, a county road that went due east and passed just north of the Ramar district. Bob had built his manor house on two hundred acres. Driving by, one could see it gleaming white and bright on top of a hill some two hundred yards away. Beyond the white plank fence bordering the road was horse pasture that covered the hill all the way up to the large brick house painted white. The sweep of the pasture was broken by a one-acre fishpond halfway up. It was a pleasant surprise to suddenly see the house on the hill after seeing only pastureland, grazing cattle, and wood lots since leaving Riverton.

The distance to the estate from the center of town was five miles, and Bob could make it to work in about fifteen minutes. His Packard could go much faster than he drove it, but he was especially careful on the narrow, twisting road. He rarely saw another car. He would occasionally come up on a mule-drawn wagon, and would get annoyed if he couldn't pass it right away.

On this particular morning he encountered three barefoot boys walking away from town, holding swimsuits and towels.

"Bet those boys are headin' for the river," Bob said to himself and waved at them as he drove by. "I loved swimmin' in that river when I was their age. Swingin' out over that cove on that vine into that cool water was great fun...almost as much fun as I had in that cove with Nadine Smith after the junior-senior prom."

But Bob was wrong. When he was a boy there had been no country estate with a swimming pool along the way.

"Geronimo!" yelled Sam as he jerked his knees up to his chest into a "cannonball." He hit the water with a ka-whump, and a huge splash threw water up and out of the pool in all directions. Carl and Butch followed him in quick succession. The boys had assumed that no one would mind them swimming in the pool. They couldn't imagine anyone letting a perfectly good swimming pool go to waste, so they had walked up the long driveway to the pool, put on their trunks behind a Muscatine grape arbor close by, and made themselves at home.

They had found out about the pool from one of the girls at school whose parents had been invited there for a Fourth of July party. The only other swimming pools the boys knew about were the one next to the city zoo and the one at Farragut Springs, both of which cost a dime to get in, money they often didn't have. Finding out about the Forrester pool had been a very welcome surprise.

Of course they sometimes swam in the river, but they preferred swimming pools. A few years before one of the older boys from Ramar drowned when the river's current was swifter than usual, following a heavy rain. He and two other boys were swinging out over the river on vines. As long as they fell close to the shore, the current had little effect on them. But the doomed boy swung out a little farther than usual and got caught by the current. He didn't swim well enough to get back to shore, and the other boys didn't dare get in the current themselves, so all they could do was helplessly run along the bank, watching him fight to stay above water. Finally he sank out of sight, and his body was found a mile downstream two days later.

Everyone in Riverton grieved for the dead boy, especially

those in the Ramar district. Even though Butch, Sam, and Carl had been little boys at the time, they had vivid memories of the incident, and every time they went to the river they were bothered by the bad memories.

The three-mile trek out Duggans Gap Road from Ramar had made them hot, thirsty and dusty. They drank from the garden hose and squirted each other before making their cannonball entry into the pool. All of the boys had learned how to swim by being thrown into the "deep end" at the city pool, so there was no danger of them drowning. They cavorted in the water, tried flips off of the diving board, and ran wide open along the sides of the pool, something the lifeguard wouldn't let them do at the city pool.

While they played, Mrs. Bob Forrester watched from an upstairs window. Jane Forrester was a self-effacing little woman who utterly deferred to her locally famous husband. For the twenty years they had been married she had been an adornment to him, something like a fancy jacket or a nice pair of Italian loafers. Her purpose in life was to make him look good. Every action she took from the moment she woke until she drifted off to sleep at night was calculated to make her husband look good. What she would wear to cocktail parties, what she would wear and serve at their dinner parties, where they would go on vacation, and what they would do there were all calculated to promote his standing in the business and social communities.

Once when she was lying out on the beach at the French Riviera, he said, "Don't get sunburned. I don't want you all splotchy when we visit the Millers at Monaco." What worried her most were the age lines creeping into her pretty, oval face, now that she was forty-two. If she hadn't been so attractive he would never have married her. She knew that if her beauty faded so would she, in all likelihood.

They had never had the children she wanted because it would "impede" his career. However, there was also the very real possibility that he had a low sperm count and couldn't bear the thought of being impotent. Once early in their marriage she had stumbled across what looked like a lab report when she was throwing out some old papers. She could see that it concerned a sperm count, but the numbers were meaningless to her. She didn't dare ask Bob about it. Now it was getting too late to start a family, so she had resigned herself to being childless.

She tolerated the boys swimming in the pool for a number of reasons. First, she was afraid to make a scene, and she hated the thought of a sheriff's deputy coming up her driveway. Second, she enjoyed their freedom vicariously, since she had none of her own.

How ironic. These boys probably don't have a dime between

them, yet they enjoy life so much. Bob and I have lots of money, and I'm miserable. And even if Bob has a mistress, as I suspect he does, I don't think he is as happy as these boys are who have nothing.... Wouldn't it be nice if they were our children? I wouldn't have any trouble at all loving boys who are so carefree and happy.

These thoughts ran through her mind as she stood at the window in her housecoat, a second cup of coffee in her hand. For just a fleeting moment the idea flashed through her head to throw the cup into the bedroom fireplace, throw off her housecoat, run to the pool in her panties and brassiere and yell "Geronimo!" as she did a cannonball into the water.

A third reason she tolerated the trespassing was that she savored the injury these boys were doing to her husband. She knew that he would be furious if he found out-—at them for trespassing, at her for not kicking them out. She liked to imagine the dirt and germs from these urchins clinging to Bob's skin, as he dog paddled around the pool, being careful not to get his thinning brown hair wet.

After they left, she put on her swim suit and went down to check the pool, to make sure they didn't leave any evidence of themselves behind, including any leaves or other debris that wouldn't normally fall in the water. To account for the wetness around the pool and on the diving board, she did a lot of splashing herself--just in case he came home unexpectedly and saw that the pool had been used.

The boys went back to Murray's house to tell him all about it. He hadn't gone with them because his mother had taken him to the dentist. Murray sat on the back steps, dejected, holding his sore jaw in his hand as his three compatriots took turns telling him about their adventure.

"I almost did a one and a half, Murray!" said Carl.

"Yeah. Almost. You coulda heard the belly flop a mile away!" Butch responded.

"At least I tried it, butt brain! You're too chicken!" Carl suggested.

"I thought I saw somebody in the upstairs winduh of the house," said Sam, "but when I rubbed the water outta my eyes to get a better look, I did'n see nothin'."

"I hadda sick in uh dennis chir," Murray mumbled through swollen, benumbed lips.

Later, after drinking some of Mrs. Austin's iced tea, all four boys resumed work on the cannon and discussed how they would humiliate the River Road Rangers once again. If they had known that none of the older boys would be fighting that year they would not have planned at all.

A Friendship Blooms
in the Greenhouse

"Mistuh Ray? Whadaya think about Jackie Robinson playin' in the Major League?" asked Jesse Carter, as Raymond Lewis strolled through the back door of the greenhouse while Jesse was watering flats of impatiens.

"I don't think it's right, Jesse. White and colored players shouldn't be playin' together." With mock seriousness, Ray continued, "For one thing, everybody knows that coloreds don't take sports serious. He might get on base, and when he's suppos'd ta be payin' close attention to the count he's libel to just start dancin' around in the infield, grinnin' like a mule eatin' briars he's so happy to be playin' with real ball players. Or [Ray grinning broadly] maybe he likes watermelon as much as you do, Jesse, and some fan throws a chunk out on the field. He's lible to run over and get it and get tagged out."

"Oh, come on, Mistuh Ray [Jesse grinning broadly], you know I don't like watermelon <u>that</u> much!"

What Raymond didn't realize but had suspected for years was that Jesse was much brighter than he let on. He had grown up not far from the greenhouse in a country shack with four other brothers and sisters. He had learned how to read when he was five and could read quite well, but as far as Raymond was concerned, he was semi-literate. Jesse understood that to survive (sometimes quite literally) you had to play elaborate games with "the man."

Now in his early thirties with a family of his own, he lived in a shack not far from his parents' place. He knew the story of Jackie Robinson quite well and followed new developments in the Riverton newspaper. He knew that the other owners were mad that Branch Rickey was going to field a black player. From conversations with his family and with members of the little Baptist church they belonged to, Jesse knew how proud the black community was of Robinson and how anxious they were for him to do well. All of them knew that blacks could play as well as whites from knowing the exploits of such black ball players as Satchel Paige and "Oh My!" Johnson, the Babe Ruth of the Negro leagues.

"What do <u>you</u> think, Jesse?"

"Well, he's a mighty fine player, I hear. But you's probly right. Niggers and whites shouldn't play on the same field."

What Raymond thought he meant was that blacks don't take the game seriously enough to be playing with the whites. What Jesse actually meant was that blacks are too good to play with whites and might one day take over all the positions.

"When you get done there I want you to come out front and help me with that load of fertilizer," Raymond said as be started down the aisle toward the front of the greenhouse.

"Yassuh!"

Raymond Lewis was not as racist as the black man assumed him to be, and much of what Ray said was not serious. Compared to many other white men in Blalock County, Ray was more progressive, but he came across as a full-fledged racist partly because of Jesse's stereotypical behavior. Thus, the nine-year relationship between these two men had been based on false assumptions about each other. Ray assumed Jesse was just another ignorant, lazy, conniving "nigra," and Jesse assumed Ray was an arrogant, greedy white "cracker."

As Ray made his way along the aisle to the front of the greenhouse, he spotted Jesse's lunch pail standing open on one of the plant tables and veered over to have a look at what he had brought for lunch. He noticed alongside a sandwich wrapped in wax paper a paperback book. He lifted it out of the lunch pail and read "*The Good Earth*, a novel by Pearl S. Buck." At the bottom was, "Complete and Unabridged."

He picked up the book and thumbed through it as he slowly walked back down the aisle to where Jesse was shutting off the water in the hose. "Jesse, what's this book I found in your lunch pail?"

Looking a little surprised, he replied, "Ah, thas jest a book I found in the garbage over to Miss Mamie's house over where my woman Annie woik. Thought I might try to make out some of the words."

"Well, you must be making out a bunch of them. I see page 104 marked with one of our plant identification cards." Jesse just stared at Ray for several seconds, with a dumbfounded look on his face. Swallowing hard, he spoke,

"I guess you better know the truth, Mr. Ray. I know how to read a lot better than I let on...In fact, I love to read. Miss Mamie told me that I would really like *The Good Earth*. It's about some starvin' Chinese peasants around the turn of the century. She was right. It's a great book. I brought it today thinkin' I might get through a page or two durin' my lunchtime. I wuz goan sit behind the tool shed so nobody could see me."

Ray, looking equally dumbfounded, replied after several seconds, "Why didn't you tell me you could read so good?"

"Mr. Ray, there ain't a lot of demand for a literate Negro unless he has a college education and can be a preacher or a teacher or somethin' like that. So I figured I wouldn't be no worse off pretendin' to be dumb. The pay would be the same. I've seen white men that were uncomfortable bein' around an educated Negro, so it seemed to be in my favor not to appear so smart."

Ray looked at him for ten seconds without speaking then said, "You've been a very good worker, and dependable. I don't care that you can read good. In fact, it might be a big help. Some of this legal mumbo jumbo I get on my desk... maybe you can help me tease out the meanin'. Why don't we just change your job description right now to Greenhouse Worker and Reader. That new title means you will get an extra fifteen cents an hour."

Jesse broke out in a large, relieved smile, "Why thank you, Mr. Ray. I'll try to read whatever you put in my face. Maybe the two of us can figure out whatever mumbo jumbo they send along."

The two men shared a chuckle as they walked to the front the greenhouse to the waiting load of fertilizer

A Racial Incident

THE FIRST DAY OF JULY was hotter and more humid than the last day of June. Crayton Turner, the Popsicle boy, was a little late getting to River Road Terrace where his sales were usually good. He liked to get there before 4:00 p.m. when the construction workers got off work. It was already 3:55, and his cotton shirt was soaked in sweat. He pedaled his cart as hard as he could to get to the work site on River Road Court where a house was under construction. When he got to Mrs. Phillips' house he was reminded of the afternoon when he and the three white boys got caught in the thunderstorm. Between gasps for air, he said to himself, "Sure could use some coolin' rain right now!"

Just as he said "coolin'" he saw a young woman in a bedroom window in the house next door to the Phillips'. The bedroom light was on, so he could see pretty well that she was undressing. It was Felicia Humphrey, wife of an Army captain stationed at Marsten Army Depot. Raised in New York City, the daughter of artists, Felicia was not in the habit--yet--of safeguarding her modesty.

Crayton was old enough to be aroused by the scene, so he slowed his cart to a stop and stared for several seconds, not fully aware of what he was doing.

Suddenly he realized a car was coming toward him and resumed pedaling down the street, hoping that the driver didn't see him looking. As he passed the car he stole a glance and was sickened to see it was a gray '39 Ford coupe splattered with mud. He knew it belonged to one of the carpenters at the construction site, a "Mr. Jewell," who wore a paint-stained pith helmet to protect his bald head from the sun. He saw the carpenter driving, another in the passenger seat, and a third in the back seat. All three were staring at him

"Wonduh whut that nigger boy was lookin' at," said Royce.

"Coulda ben mos'anything," said Jim. "That boy talks a streak. Almos' forgits to collect for his Popsicles."

"Well, lookit that!" yelled Royce, as the car stopped in front of the Phillips' house. The other two men looked back to see Mrs. Humphrey smoothing out the wrinkles and straightening the waist of a light blue sundress she had just pulled over her head.

"That nigger's been eyeballin' a naked white woman!" yelled Royce. "Let's git 'im!"

Crayton saw the stopped car and heard the yelling, so he pedaled as hard as he could toward the Jewish golf course at the end of the road. He was heading for the wild privet hedge at the edge of the rough. By the time Jewell got the car turned around in Mrs. Phillips' driveway and sped back down the street, Crayton had already left the street and was frantically pedalling down the fairway toward the hedge. He was afraid his lungs would burst.

The bicycle cart smashed through the hedge and got wedged in a tangle of limbs and vines. Just as he jumped from the cart and leaped the short, rusty, barbed wire fence, the car slid to a stop, and the three men plunged into the hedge after him. Crayton didn't know where he was. He just knew that River Road and houses were straight ahead, so he ran as hard as he could, ignoring the blackberry briars and wild plum thorns that scratched him and tore at his clothes.

Crayton knew the fate of black men who were even suspected of lusting after a white woman and was terrified that they wanted to lynch him or castrate him or both. The fact that he was only a boy didn't give him any relief from his panic. He had never been so terrified in his life. All he could hear was the sound of the men crashing through the bushes behind him, the heavy thumping of his heart, and his gasping for air.

Dead ahead he saw a chicken house on his left and a cluster of peach trees on his right. In a few seconds he was at the top of the back steps pounding the door with both fists. Ruthelle jerked it open.

"Whatchew wont, boy!"

Crayton felt great relief seeing a brown face, even though it was scowling. "Sum white men are chasin' me! Please let me in!"

Ruthelle looked up to see three dirty, sweaty white men walking past the chicken house into the back yard. She quickly pulled Crayton behind her and filled the door with her body. Even though Crayton was almost as tall as Ruthelle, she seemed much bigger to the terrified boy. The men stopped in front of the steps.

"Wench, that there nigger boy behind yo' back's ben

gawkin' at a naked white woman!" said Royce, clenching and unclenching his fists. "We aim to have a little talk with 'im!"

Ruthelle stood as tall as she could and mustered all of her courage. If any of them made the slightest move she would slam and lock the door. But until they did she wanted to try talking to them.

"I'll have you know that <u>Doctor</u> Peter Flournoy, the Blalock County school superintendent's goan be home soon, and he ain't goan like all this goins on one bit! This here is a <u>boy</u>! He's too young to be lookin' at no women! You big men got no bidness chasin' this boy!" As she yelled her lower lip trembled.

"We ain't arguin' witchew, gal!" said Jim. "We seen the whole thing! He wuz stopped in front of her house justa lookin', but when he seen us he took off!"

"We don't aim to hurt him none," said Jewell, in a more soothing tone. "We jes wanna make sure he unerstands where he can and cannot aim his eyes. We all know that boy. He sells us Popsicles at the construction site. We jes wont him to do <u>right</u>!" Addressing the small brown hand clinging to Ruthelle's waist, Jewell continued," Boy! I don't evuh wont to see you or hear of you lookin' at no white girl or woman! You unerstand me!?"

"Yassuh," Crayton whimpered from behind Ruthelle.

With that Jewell turned on his heel and marched back past the chicken house, and the other two followed. Royce looked back scowling and mumbling.

Ruthelle slowly closed the door and turned to Crayton. A great sadness filled her eyes. "What's yo name, boy?"

"Crayton, ma'am"

"Crayton whut?"

"Turner, ma'am"

"Crayton Turner Ma'am, you're old enough to know how to act around white folks. Don't you know what white crackers do to black men who look at white women?"

"Yes'm, I know, but I jes forgot. I aint <u>never</u> goan forgit agin!"

"I felt you tremblin' against my back, so I do believe you've had a good scare—-and a good lesson! Those men said you sell Popsicles. Well, I want you to bring me a Popsicle from time to time so I can see how you're gettin' along. But I can't afford more'n a couple a week, so don't you be comin' everyday. Where is yo' cart now?"

"It's back there in those bushes," Crayton said, pointing his long arm and finger at the back of the lot.

"I want you to sit down over there at the kitchen table and drink a glass of ice tea. When Mr. Flournoy gits home shortly, I'll tell him what happened and aks him to go with you to git the cart in case those men are hangin' around."

She walked to the refrigerator and got Crayton his tea. As she poured the cold, dark liquid, she watched the clear condensation form on the outside of the glass, a cold sweat.

A Cowboy Misadventure

"I'm Gene Autry!" yelled Todd.

"I'm Roy Rogers!" yelled Graham.

"I want to be Roy Rogers," whined Blake.

"You can be the Lone Ranger," offered Graham.

Blake didn't look especially satisfied with the idea but saw no better alternative to being Roy Rogers, the favorite of both him and Graham. *I'll just have to yell quicker next time* he decided, as he took his cap pistol out of its holster and tried spinning it on his finger.

All of the boys had gotten cap pistols in a cardboard holster for Christmas, along with a few boxes of caps. Blake had also got a new, red, straw cowboy hat, so his looked newer than the two straw-colored ones worn by the other two boys. Graham was also wearing a kerchief around his neck. He had taken one of Susan's "old" silk kerchiefs and wound it tightly into a roll then wrapped it around his neck with the knot on the side, in the style the "King of the Cowboys" wore his. The effect might have been attractive if the kerchief had not been so large.

While standing on the back steps of the Flournoy house, Blake saw Spot, a solid black mongrel that had taken up with the Armisteads several months earlier. He twirled his pistol back into its holster then drew it as fast as he could, aimed it at Spot and snapped off three caps in quick succession. Spot flinched at the first pop but then just stared quizzically at Blake. The acrid gunpowder smoke released by the popping of the caps swirled around the heads of the boys and slightly burned their nostrils and eyes. This prompted Todd and Graham to draw their pistols and start firing at Spot. The dog then decided that retreat was in order and loped past the chicken house into the back field. What was referred to as the chicken house hadn't housed any chickens for several years.

As soon as he was no longer an interesting target the three boys began shooting at each other and running for cover. When Graham darted behind the brick barbecue pit, Blake ran to the corner of the chicken house, and Todd ran behind the pecan tree. For the next several minutes the battle raged. Graham liked the sound of ricocheting bullets he had heard in a Roy Rogers movie, so he tried imitating the sound of imaginary bullets ricocheting off the barbecue, "Kuh-ching!"

"Let's play like we're partners chasin' outlaws!" yelled Todd, who had tired of all his bullets ricocheting. When he stepped away from the tree, Graham sprang up and shot at him three times.

"I need a mask," said Blake as he strolled over from the chicken house. "The Lone Ranger has a black mask."

"Maybe you could be the Lone Ranger while he was still a Texas Ranger," suggested Graham, the local authority on Western heroes.

"I don't want to be the Not-Alone-Yet Ranger," groused Blake. "I want a mask."

"I know where some black paint is," offered Todd. "We could paint one on 'im."

While Blake was considering this offer, Graham accepted it for him, "Yeah! That should do the trick!"

The three boys then ran over to the garage of Todd's house. While Graham and Blake waited outside, Todd tiptoed into the garage, so as not to arouse his mother, who might be in the kitchen. He found the small can of black paint and the brush his father had used to touch up the wrought-iron railing on the small front porch and tiptoed back out to his friends.

They then raced over to the Flournoy chicken house and

sat on the concrete floor. Todd used a penny he had in his pocket to open the can then stirred the paint with the handle of the brush. Ignoring the paint he got on his fingers when he grasped the handle, Todd dipped the brush in the paint.

"Take your hat off so I can see what I'm doin!" said Todd while eyeing the area around Blake's eyes. Blake took off his hat and held still while Todd gingerly dabbed paint in his eyebrows then all around each eye. While Todd painted, Graham inspected his handiwork carefully, offering occasional suggestions. After five minutes the mask was finished. To somebody else, the "mask" might look like two severe black eyes, but to Graham and Todd, the black mask against Blake's cotton blond hair made a striking image.

After putting his red cowboy hat back on his head, Blake drew his pistol, shot Graham and Todd and ran out the door. Graham and Todd drew their pistols and chased after him. For the next ten minutes Blake was in a running gun battle with the other two boys until his eyes began to sting from the paint fumes. It soon got so bad that he began crying and ran home.

When he burst into the house, and Marsha saw him, she had to steady herself on the telephone stand. Her boy's beautiful blue eyes were rimmed in red from the irritation then surrounded by black.

"What in the world happened to you, Blake!" she yelled before recovering herself and reaching for her son.

"We wuz just playin' cowboys, Mama!" blubbered Blake, who then cried louder when he rubbed his eye with his fist.

"Don't touch your face!" Marsha cried while closely examining Todd's handiwork. "Who painted your face this way?"

"Todd and Gra-ham. They wuz makin' me a Lone Ranger ma-ask," Todd blubbered between gasps.

Marsha had him close his eyes tightly while she removed the paint with turpentine and washed the skin with a soapy washcloth. Then she had him rinse his eyes several times with tap water in a glass eyecup. Finally she rubbed hand cream into the skin around his eyes. When she was satisfied that she had done enough to protect his eyes, she got on the phone and called the mothers of the other two boys.

That evening Graham got a stern talking to by his parents, who took turns talking. They knew from past experience that such talks were sufficient to discipline Graham. What he mainly needed to understand was that paint can damage eyes. Todd's parents weren't so "progressive." When Ruby told Raymond what had happened, he told Todd to go outside and cut a "good-size switch. And it better be good size!" Todd ambled out into the yard with his father's pocket knife and cut a three-foot long, quarter-inch thick, privet hedge branch. He then pulled off all the leaves on his way back to the house. Raymond then took him to his room and used the hefty switch to impress on Todd the error of his ways.

Professor Fremont
Comes Calling

"Who is it!?" shouted Ruth, in a slightly quaking voice. The doorbell had startled her, since it was rarely used. Only after the second ring did she realize what it was and make her way to the front door and peer through the sidelight.

"It's Gayle Fremont, ma'am! My car boiled over coming up the hill! I'm afraid I've got a busted thermostat! Haven't been servicing it like I should! Do you mind if I use your telephone to call a garage!?"

Ruth peered at him intently through the sidelight. "Aren't you colored!?"

"...Well, I suppose I am," he said resignedly. "I don't think so, but living here in Riverton has made me live like I'm colored, whatever that means!"

Thus went the initial exchange between Ruth St. John and

the first middle-class black person she had ever seen. Gayle Fremont was on a short vacation from his professorship at St. Luke College. He was on his way to spend some time with his parents in New Orleans. Nattily dressed in a white linen suit and a straw hat, Gayle was a light-skinned Negro who sometimes passed as white, but he considered that a form of hypocrisy and usually took his place among the other people deemed colored. A young man with a Ph.D. from Johns Hopkins University, he chafed under the Jim Crow laws he grew up under in New Orleans and now in Riverton. He had resolved to leave the South first chance he got and take a position in a northern college or university.

To avoid getting trapped into living under Jim Crow laws he avoided all entanglements with women who were determined to stay in the South with their relatives.

"You'll have to come around to the back!" Ruth shouted through the glass. "I'll have to make the call for you! I can't let you come in the house!" Being used to the insults, Gayle just shrugged and made his way around to the back where he stood outside the closed door.

After getting the number of the garage that services "colored cars" and making the call for him, she walked to the back door and shouted at him through the glass,"They said they can be here in about half an hour! Do you want a glass of ice wahter!?"

"Yes, ma'am! That would be very refreshing on a hot day like this!" After handing him the frosty glass, she pulled the door wide open and closely examined him from head to toe. Gayle just stood there smiling and sipping the water. "How is it that you dress so well and speak so well?" Ruth asked.

Gayle's eyebrows rose slightly in surprise. He suddenly realized that each of them had things to learn about the other. The world of his upbringing had been solid black middle class. His father was a highly successful insurance executive, and his mother was the daughter of a minister of a very large African Methodist Episcopal church. Even though New Orleans had genteel whites like the St. Johns, he had never had contact with them, and had not learned much about them in getting his college degrees.

"My mother always dressed me nicely. Everyone I grew up with dressed nicely. We even wore bibs so we wouldn't get watermelon juice on our nice clothes." As soon as he made the sarcastic remark, he regretted it. To him, she was just a child in many ways. It was unfair of him to take advantage of her naivete' "My parents in New Orleans are very fortunate. They both come from solid middle class families and raised me in one. I was given an excellent grade school education and then sent off to college. Last year I completed my Ph.D. in geology at Johns Hopkins." Smiling brightly, he continued, "I've always loved rocks."

Ruth just stood there, her mouth slightly open. After an embarrassing few seconds, she responded, "I've never known anybody with a Ph.D." Now it was her turn to regret what she said, so she smiled, too, and looked down at the floor. "Won't you come in and rest awhile, Jail?"

"Gayle. G, A, Y, L, E"

"I'm sorry. Gayle. That's a pretty name."

Gayle entered her kitchen and sat down at the kitchen table, where they sipped ice water and talked about the strange new world both had discovered. When the wrecker came, Ruth asked him to stop by after his car was fixed to talk some more. After he left she momentarily regretted inviting him because of what the neighbors might think if they saw him, but then she decided the neighbors could just talk if they wanted to. She had enjoyed talking to the nice young man. But just to be on the safe side, she would have him come around to the back when he got there.

As he bumped along in the passenger seat of the old wrecker, Gayle reflected on what had transpired between him and the old lady. Then he realized that he hadn't gotten her name.

Probably just as well. She might think I was 'uppity' if I asked her name. On the other hand we did have a very nice conversation. At times I felt like I was a visitor from another planet and in some ways I was. My world is certainly alien to her. Not that I am all that familiar with her world either. I think I know more about her than she does about me, but I sure was surprised when she asked about my clothes. If all she has ever known are these feet shuffling old uncles and aunties or these illiterate country bumpkins I see moseying along the road, I can better understand her bigotry. I am going to stop by on my way back out and visit with her a while longer... Uh Oh! Something I haven't thought about. What if I make her upset and she screams for the neighbors or calls the police and tells them I tried to rape her? I would be dangling from the end of a rope by sunset--and she acted like she could use the services of a man....Now listen to you, Gayle! You're acting like a bigot yourself. She's just a sweet, innocent little old white lady. You should be flattered that she invited you to come back. That's got to be the first social invitation she has ever offered to a Negro. And I bet she will invite me to come in the front door and sit in the parlor. I think we're both getting an education out of this.

Warmly satisfied with his resolve to see her again, he smiled as the wrecker pulled into the garage. A change of thermostats and a replenishment of water and anti-freeze for the radiator of his '38 Ford and Gayle was on his way to his River Road rendezvous.

"Gayle! Come in!" said Ruth as she grabbed him by the elbow and quickly pulled him into the foyer. "I'm so glad you could come back." She continued talking rapidly and nervously as she led him down the hallway to the kitchen. She offered him the seat he used before.

"Do you like ice tea? Would you like some lemon in it?" she said as she bustled about the kitchen. "Germaine told me that you people like ice tea as much as white people do. She makes me a large pitcher of it every time she is here. I've got some teacakes also. Not as good as the ones Mrs. Baxter used to make, but they're all right. I..."

"Ma'am, I'd love some iced tea. We drink an ocean of it in New Orleans every summer. Lemon also, thank you."

"I'm sorry, Gayle. I guess I was babbling," she said with her back to him as she poured the tea into the tall glasses. "I'm sure you can understand how starved for conversation someone can be, especially with someone knowledgeable like you. And you don't have to keep calling me 'Ma'am,' my name is Ruth St. John. Miss St. John."

Ruth and Gayle enjoyed an hour of genial conversation, sipping ice tea. Gayle had two glasses then nature called. He hesitated to ask to use her bathroom but eventually did. Ruth also hesitated granting him permission--not because she was insensitive but because it was such an unusual situation for her. When her maid was there the question was never asked. Germaine would just find a discreet time to slip into the bathroom. She and Ruth just pretended she didn't have bodily functions.

Even though Ruth knew on an intellectual level that there were educated teachers, ministers, doctors and businessmen, she never acknowledged them on a personal level. They were just out there someplace, as though on another planet. When whites <u>did</u> encounter educated blacks they resisted acknowledging their elevated status by calling them by their first name. This kept the distance necessary to preserve the illusion of racial inequality. Even the Reverend Doctor Willis Ranger was called "Willis" by all whites he had contact with. His role as pastor of Spring Street Baptist Church, with the largest black congregation in Riverton, gave him no special consideration. The church was on the western edge of the campus of St. Luke's college where Gayle taught, so Gayle had been over several times to hear him preach, and found him to be learned and eloquent.

What Gayle learned from their encounter was that even though Ruth was clearly a racist, she did not hate blacks. His experience growing up in New Orleans had shown him that whites in the South don't hate blacks. They genuinely love blacks they know well--but only if the blacks stay in their place. For whatever reason, whites were very threatened by any talk of racial equality. He also came to realize that in some ways blacks were better off in the South because in the North many whites were hypocritical. In the South you at least knew where you stand--and Gayle enjoyed gently challenging the status quo.

He also learned that black prejudice is just as bad as white prejudice. Some blacks he knew referred to whites as "honkies" and "crackers." Ruth, despite her racism, was an individual. Yes, she was a product of her culture, but she was also a fair-minded, intelligent, rather well educated human being who wanted to bridge the gap between them.

"Gayle, is it true that colored men lust after white women?"

After reflecting on her question for several seconds, he said, "I don't think so. I for one don't. I much prefer the smooth bronze skin and other attributes of colored people. I prefer a woman that looks like me. White people, if you don't mind me saying so, look bleached. Their thin lips and thin noses look...inadequate, like they are underdeveloped. I hope I'm not offending you, Miss Ruth, but I just wanted to give you my honest answer." Gayle blinked a couple of times, looking slightly embarrassed, and took a couple of quick sips of his tea.

"I'm not at all offended, Gayle. I can understand your point of view. We whites think the opposite of coloreds. We think your skin is too dark, and your lips and noses are too thick. We think someone like you--who looks half-white--is more attractive, because you look more like us."

Feeling they had reached a comfortable familiarity with each other by this point, Ruth looked hard at this young man who could be her grandson and asked him a rather personal question,

"Gayle, I hope you don't mind me asking, but do you have any white blood?"

Gayle was now feeling the same level of familiarity and answered, "Yes, my father's grandfather was a white man. He was a planter in sugar cane country in southern Louisiana, and he took my great grandmother as a mistress. My grandfather was their only child. He was raised as a slave, but when Freedom came he left his mother, who stayed on the plantation, and traveled to New Orleans where he got a grade school education and ran a very successful livery stable. He married a local girl. They had five children, and one of the boys was my father, who got a better education than he got. Then I came along and couldn't get enough schooling." Gayle broke into a big smile. "They had to finally run me off."

Ruth told him about living in the city until her grandmother died then her family moving to the Aldrich homestead. She told him what she knew about her grandfather, Rem Aldrich, the slaves he had, and how he treated them. She was careful to make sure he understood that he never had a colored mistress. Gayle wondered how she could know that for sure.

In the course of their conversation they developed a deep respect for each other and were both surprised by how much it had changed their perspective on race relations. Although an open friendship would be impossible for them, they both hoped for additional opportunities to talk.

Nathan Armistead, Witch Doctor

AT SEVEN O'CLOCK ONE MORNING, just as Nathan arrived at the site of one of the houses under construction, he was approached by Tom Neeley, the black foreman of the laborers working for Barney Rogers, the general contractor for the development.

"Mistuh Nathan," if you got a few minutes to tawlk I need to tell you 'bout one of my boys."

"What's the problem, Tom?"

"Rufus Brown be one of my best woikers, but he aint been at woik for the last coupla days. I went over to where he stay with his mama, and foun' him sittin' on the front poach. When I aks him how come he aint been at woik, he told me he just got married. I sayd, 'That aint no reason to quit woik! Yo' woman's goan be there when you get home!

139

That poontang don't go bad if it aint used! In fact, it gets better!' Ise hopin' he might like my jokin' around and laugh with me, but he kept a dead serious face the whole time. Then he sayd, 'Louise wont go in the shack Mr. Parker give us to live in. Sez it's hainted. Sez she's heard stories all her life 'bout that place. Caint nobody talk sense to her. She convinced the haints goan scare us to death if we spend one night in that place. I looked for us another place to live, but they aint none.' Tell you the truth, Mistuh Nathan, I hates to lose a good woiker. And he jest got married. Mistuh Rogers say to let him go, but I hates to do that..."

"Let me think on that, Tom, and I'll let you know something tomorrow."

That night, while Nathan watched Marsha Louise finish making supper, with Janie and Blake not yet home, Nathan raised the problem with his wife.

"It's hard to believe that in the middle of the twentieth century there are still people who can be so superstitious," he said.

"It's not surprising to me," Marsha replied, while stirring the onions and calf's liver in the skillet. "While she was busy trying to make me into a lady, our maid Flossie would tell me how important it was to get a good education. She told me about coloreds she knew or knew of who wuz as dumbstruck superstitious as that girl. She talked about voodoo dolls, castin' spells, and all such as that. She told about one woman who collected every strand of her hair when it was cut for fear somebody might get a strand or two and cast a spell on her."

"Did she say anything about what to do about it?"

"All I remember her saying is that sometimes a "spell" was broken by a 'witch doctor,' usually an old, old woman, who would stand over the "victim" and speak some mumbo jumbo while sprinkling some kind of foul smelling liquid on his head."

"What about a 'hainted' house?"

"Same sort of thing. She would just stalk around in some kind of ceremonial way and sprinkle that stuff on tables, chairs, walls, and so forth," Marsha said, while making a short ceremonial dance in front of her stove. "Why don't you dress up in a witch doctor outfit and go cast out those ghosts yourself?" she said teasingly.

They both chuckled at the thought, but Nathan began seriously considering the possibility. Maybe he could put some of his architect's tools in a bag and tell Louise that these are modern scientific instruments for ridding houses of ghosts. He could pull out his slide rule and show her all the numbers and symbols and began sliding the parts back and forth while chanting something.

The next morning he arrived at the construction site with

a croaker sack filled with a slide rule, two T-squares, old blueprints, and as many other foreign-looking objects he could lay his hands on, but he was only half convinced he should go through with his plan. As soon as he drove up, he saw Tom walking rapidly toward him, a big grin on his face.

"Mistuh Nathan, Rufus at woik today. Yonder he is up there wif thuh roofers."

"What happened?"

"Rufus mama know a lady who know a lady who know a spell-bustin' old woman name of Awnt Bessie down near Willow Spring. She come yestiddy and went through that house wif Rufus and Louise and casted out all those haints. Louise happy as a dead pig in the sunshine now."

"I'm so glad to hear that, Tom," said Nathan as he quietly slid his hand over the jeep seat to make sure his croaker sack was closed.

That night, after the children were in bed, Nathan and Marsha listened to *The Inner Sanctum* on the radio. While listening to the spooky drama, Nathan was reminded of the incident with Rufus and Louise and wondered if white people are any more sophisticated if they can be titillated by ghost stories. He wondered how many mature and "rational" white people would spend the night alone in a house believed to be haunted.

After turning off the radio, Nathan asked Marsha if she could spend the night alone in a haunted house. Marsha continued knitting for a few seconds before responding, "Hmmm. That's a good question. Are you asking me this because of what happened to those coloreds?"

"Yeah, partly, and also because you and I enjoy being scared by spooky radio shows. I just want to know how much difference there is between us and Rufus and Louise."

"There's a lot of difference and you know it, Nathan. We're educated and they're not. And much more important, we're white and they're colored. We would handle a haunted house situation with a lot more...uh...dignity. Did you know that Miss Ruth across the road says she has ghosts in her old house?"

"No, I didn't."

"Early last spring I knocked on her door while collecting for the March of Dimes, and she invited me in for a cup of tea. Her sister as you know died just a month or so before that, so I was careful not to say the wrong things. Well, she was in a talkative mood and began telling me about noises she couldn't explain. She said that she's been hearing strange noises at night since she was a little girl, but now they were occurring in the daytime.

Most of the time she could explain them away as settlin' of the old house or flyin' squirrels in the attic, but only a day or two before that she was washin' a few dishes in her sink when she heard the front door open and close. She dried off her hands and walked into the hallway and toward the front rooms. She guessed it might be Cousin Bea or Harvey and she just didn't hear the doorbell. But when she got to the front she didn't see anybody. Not in the parlor or in the dining room. When she tried the front door she found it was locked.

Then she heard distinct footsteps in the hallway behind her. They were going toward the back of the house. She turned quickly but saw nothing. Then she heard the kitchen door to the outside open and close." Having gotten rather wound up in her narration at this point, Marsha dropped a stitch and had to fumble with it. "Er...then she walked to the kitchen door, opened it, and got a glimpse of a figure as it rounded the corner of her old chicken house. She said she couldn't tell anything about it except that it seemed to be inside a cloud or a fog of some kind.

She said it scared her, but the main difference between Miss Ruth and the colored girl is that Miss Ruth looks for logical explanations first. The girl looks for ghosts first. When I talked to Miss Ruth, she hadn't come up with an explanation yet, but she was working on it. "Might have something to do with losing Rachael," she said. The important thing is that the old woman didn't leave her house. She stayed there. She believes that there is a logical explanation for what happened. It's just a matter of time before she figures it out."

Nathan pondered what she said, then, rising slowly from his overstuffed chair and stretching, he replied, "You might be right, Marsha." But as he closed up for the night he thought about what she had said and decided that since he knew of "colored" architects in the North the difference between Louise and Miss Ruth had more to do with education than with race.

Intimations of Mortality

JANE FORRESTER WAS THINKING ABOUT death. It started when she picked up a cardboard fan someone had left on top of the magazines in her doctor's office. The ceiling fan was simply moving around the hot air in the waiting room, so she picked up the hand fan to get some cool air to her face. She was afraid that melting makeup would make her look like a clown. To make sure her hair at least was nice Jane took out her brush and stroked the thick, gray-streaked, blond tresses that touched her shoulders. After putting the hairbrush back in her purse, she pulled at the hem of her floral print sundress to make sure it wasn't bunched anyplace.

Satisfied that her thick hair was smooth, she noticed on one side of the paper fan an advertisement for Marshall's Funeral Home. She read it over several times. Jane had been feeling especially fragile and mortal in recent weeks. First it was aches and pains she didn't recognize. Then came occasional hot flashes she had never had before. When she talked to her mother about her symptoms, her mother mentioned something about "going through the change." All of this distressed her a great deal because in her mind it signaled the beginning of the end of her life.

She hated that thought because her whole life had been devoted to beginning her life. As a child she chafed under the restrictions imposed on her as a debutante-in-training. She had to dress in crinolines and lace and join other little girls for tea parties with their dolls. Many times she would have preferred climbing trees with her brother. She consoled herself with the idea that life would be much better for her once she had her "coming out." But that was not the case. She was controlled even more.

As a young girl she had to attend the Emily Minton School, when she would have preferred public school. After her debut they enrolled her in the Florence Hennessey College for Women, when she would rather have attended the University of Alabama. After college she looked forward to marriage and getting away from her parents and grandparents, but that was also a big disappointment. Bob turned out to be like another father, but with disgusting sexual appetites.

What did she have to look forward to now? A steady

transformation into a scrunched up, hump-backed old crone with yellow teeth? This last mental image reminded her of the Wolf Man movies in which Lon Chaney, Jr. grows hair on his face and his teeth become fangs. She didn't care for those Frankenstein/Dracula/Wolf Man movies, but her husband did, so they went. Now, here she sat, waiting to see her gynecologist about her incipient menopause. Her mother had talked to her about "the change," as had aunts and older girlfriends. What she learned was that there wasn't much medical science could do about it. When a woman finally gets rid of menstrual cramps she gets hot flashes--and worse.

The longer she sat and thought about her future, the angrier she became. In this so-called free country she had enjoyed no freedom. She might as well have been a slave for all the decisions she had been allowed to make. Ever since she first realized she was on the brink of menopause, ending forever any chance that she could become a mother, her mood had grown increasingly more sour. Observing the boys frolic in her swimming pool had been one of the worst of those days, for she could imagine herself as their mother, lying on a chaise lounge next to the pool watching them play.

After they left and she was disguising their visit by splashing in the pool herself and removing tell-tale trash, she reflected on how many children had ever been invited to swim in the pool and realized that there had been none. In fact, she couldn't remember more than two or three times in her whole married life that children had been in their house.

Shifting her weight in the chair to get more comfortable, she reflected on her childless life and realized that this day was <u>the</u> worst of all those bad days. She was becoming so distraught that she was afraid of breaking down in front of a waiting room full of patients. So she slowly stood and calmly walked toward the door. As she approached the door, she stared at the frosted glass and became aware that her life had become as gray and opaque as the glass.

She walked down the stairs to the street and entered her car, where she sat for a few minutes trying to get control of herself. While sitting there she felt a great calm settle over her, and her face become a sober mask. She decided to do what she had fantasized about doing for months.

She started her car, drove to the bank and emptied out her bank account of $2865.86. Bob gave her $5000 a month to handle all household expenses. She rarely spent all of it because Bob was the one who defined "household expenses," so she had to be prepared for unexpected items. She told the bank clerk that they had a sudden need for a large amount of cash and would replace it soon, so she left $5.00 in the account to keep it open. She didn't want the bank manager to get concerned and call Bob at his office.

She then drove to the travel agency they used and asked for some brochures of Caribbean destinations. She and Bob, she told them, had always wanted to vacation in one of the less known destinations, so could they recommend some truly out-of-the-way places to one of their best customers? She left with several brochures and a few hand written descriptions and hand drawn maps of obscure islands. She also left instructions for the agent to call their house if she came up with any other ideas, hoping Bob would get the call.

Jane had no intention of going to the Caribbean. She was going to Lawrence Refuge, a small island off the coast of Nova Scotia. When she was sixteen she met a distant cousin her age who had grown up there. Her cousin's stories about the sea storms and rough-hewn fishermen fascinated her. As life with Bob grew more depressing, she thought increasingly more about the village, and what it would take to live there.

She decided she would arrive as a widow who needed to get away from reminders of her beloved late husband. She would conserve her cash while looking for work in one of the shops or maybe on the waterfront. She might even apply to work on a fishing vessel of some kind. She learned that fishing boat crews make good money. Maybe she could even one day become a Canadian citizen so she could have a pension in her old age. Any claims to American

Social Security were out of the question since her husband had far reaching connections, and he would be implacably furious at her for leaving <u>him</u>. His disgrace would be almost intolerable. Even though she would not leave him a goodbye note, she was sure he would claim she did, perhaps saying that she loved him intensely but couldn't bear to have him see her waste away with, say, cancer. She knew Bob only too well.

She would hurry home and pack a few things, put on some traveling clothes, and then drive to Mobile, where she would stay in a hotel that night. The next day she would sell the car, again as an aggrieved widow, then take a cab to the airport for a flight to New York City. There she would board a ship for Nova Scotia. During one of her fantasies about leaving Bob, she had gone to the Montgomery Public Library and learned that ships serving the Maritime Provinces departed regularly from New York Harbor.

All of these details were thought out while she drove out Duggans Gap Road to their estate. When she arrived she felt better than she had in a long time and actually had a spring in her step as she walked up the stairs to her bedroom. When she saw her widowed mother's picture on her dresser, she realized how narrow and self-centered her concerns had been. All that she could think about was herself and Bob. She paced back and forth across the large bedroom carpet trying to decide what to do. Finally she made up her mind that she couldn't afford to say anything either to her mother or her brother, because they couldn't be trusted to keep the information from Bob. As much as she regretted it, she decided to make a clean break.

In addition to packing a couple of suitcases with clothes, she emptied out her jewelry box. She had diamond pendants, a diamond encrusted watch, and gold brooches, necklaces and bracelets. She then took from Bob's dresser gold cufflinks, gold tie clasps, and two diamond stickpins. She took from her closet a mink stole and a full-length chinchilla coat. All this would be her reserve in case she needed money later on. She felt sure she could sell the items at a good price in Montreal.

Dressed in a smart, light blue business suit, nylon stockings and black heels, she began carrying the suitcases down the staircase. When she almost twisted her ankle on the first trip she kicked off the heels and made the second trip in her stocking feet. She chuckled to consider what Bob's reaction would be when he finds her gone.

She expected he would burst into the house in his usual, imperious way and shout like he usually does: "Jane! Martini! Pool! Now!" as he stripped off his clothes and dumped them on the living room furniture. On many occasions she would bring his very dry martini, made to exact specifications, and find him in a chaise lounge in his underwear. Without even looking at her he would taste it and tell her if "it'll do." Once he threw an unsatisfactory martini, glass and all, into the pool and ordered her to bring him another one "made for me."

As she drove back to Riverton she entertained herself by imagining what his behavior would be when he got home that day.

"Jane! Martini! Made for <u>me</u>! After making himself comfortable in his lounge chair he would grow impatient when she wasn't there within a couple of minutes. "Damn it, Jane! Where are you? I've had a really bad day!" When that got no response, he would curse under his breath as he stalked back to the kitchen, where she was supposed to be this time of day. When he didn't find her there he would go to the bottom of the stairs and bellow up to the bedroom.

This sort of thing would go on until he realized she was not in the house or on the grounds and had not left a note. He would then call her mother, whom he normally avoids like a disease, only to discover she knows nothing. Would he ever start worrying about her? Now that's a question she would love to know the answer to. He had never shown any genuine concern for her welfare. But she will just have to be content to speculate. When would he call the police? Probably soon after talking to her mother, she surmised.

This delicious enactment of his likely reactions kept Jane so thoroughly entertained that she almost missed her turn onto the Mobile Highway and had to swerve sharply. Cruising smoothly in her maroon Lincoln Continental convertible, her hair tossed by the wind, she looked at her watch and saw that it was only 2:00 p.m. Since she felt really good, she decided to continue on to New Orleans rather than stop in Mobile. She realized that Bob was just relentless enough to check out all airports close by before she could make her getaway. She smiled, sucked in a lung full of freedom, floored the accelerator, and lurched into a new life, where she would finally begin to live.

A Death in the Family

THE FLOURNOYS' PET DOG RUFUS was about fourteen years old that summer. No one knew for sure exactly how old he was since he had just taken up with them one day when he was just a big puppy. Harold was taking out the garbage for his mother when he saw the dog standing near the garbage can staring at him and licking his mouth at the sight and smell of fried chicken scraps. Harold called to his mother, and they both melted with pity for the dirty, skinny little dog.

Trying to determine his pedigree would have been futile, but it didn't matter because he was as lovable as he was homely and soon became a member of the family. Everywhere the children went in the neighborhood Rufus was close behind. When Graham was born four years later, the dog was a good-sized mongrel with brown and white fur. With an oversized brown and white head and small black eyes rimmed in pink, Rufus had a comical appearance that complemented his very gentle disposition. He would let the toddler Graham climb on his back and try to ride him. Since the dog was in the house a great deal of the time, Anna made the children give him a bath at least once a month.

Anna and Pete made sure Rufus got his rabies shot every year and checked him often for fleas and ticks. On one occasion Maxine showed her dad a gray tick engorged with blood. It was about the size of a grape. Using a box of stick matches, Pete would strike one and while the phosphorous was still burning blow it out and put the hot matchstick against the tick. After a few of these burns the tick backed out and Pete grabbed him with a tissue. He told the children as they watched in wide-eyed wonder that the reason he didn't just pull out the tick was because its head would pop off and stay in the skin, which could cause an infection. The boys found the explanation fascinating; the girls were repulsed.

Early in the summer of 1947, the aged Rufus was arthritic but did his best to keep up with Graham, Todd, and Blake. They even took him up into the tree house one day, but they never tried it again. It took all three of them to get the fifty-pound dog up the tree. As they struggled and sweated, lifting him and pushing him, he whimpered but never cried out. Once up in the tree he kept his tail between his legs and his ears laid back. The boys understood that he didn't enjoy being in the tree house.

A few days later Anna became so concerned about his slow, painful movements that she called their veterinarian, Dr. Brown, whose clinic was in downtown Riverton. The doctor said he wanted to keep him for a couple of days and try some remedies. On the third day the doctor's assistant, Mary, called to say that Rufus was feeling much better, and was moving about almost normally. The whole family was relieved to hear he was doing so much better. Anna even called Harold and Maxine long distance to tell them the good news. A few hours later, Mary called to say that when the kennel boy opened his cage to put down his food, the boy turned his back for a second and Rufus jumped out of his cage and loped out the back door. He and Mary ran after him, but he disappeared quickly down the alley and through a gap in the wooden fence. The family's euphoria turned to dread and worry.

Since his previous vet, now retired, had been both a large and small animal doctor, his office had been out in the country close to the cattle and horses he cared for. Their current vet, Dr. Brown, was a small animal specialist downtown, and Rufus had never been to his office before, so the family knew he was four miles away in a totally strange place. Pete and Graham got into Pete's Ford coupe and drove into town to look for him. But they shouldn't have been so concerned. Like all dogs, Rufus had the homing instinct and arrived back home a little over an hour after he escaped. Susan saw him limping along their driveway. He was hot and very thirsty but seemed to be okay otherwise. Dr. Brown just gave them the medicines and salves he had been using, and the family continued the treatments themselves.

One morning late in June Rufus was unable to rise from the large, soft dog bed Anna had made for him. Every effort produced a pitiable whimper. Every effort of theirs to help him get up made his pain worse. Looking into his eyes, everyone, even Nancy, could see that the old dog was ready to depart his painful life. Pete called his office and told them he would be in later that day and then called for a family conference. It was soon agreed that Rufus should be put to sleep, so amid the anguished crying of Graham, Maxine and Nancy, Anna and Pete left Ruthelle in charge and took Rufus to the vet's office.

Soon the deed was done, and Rufus was put in a cardboard box and loaded into the trunk of the Oldsmobile for burial at home. While Pete drove slowly along, a tear traced its way down a wrinkle in his face. He remarked, "I hope that if I get that way you'll have me put to sleep, too."

ROUGHNECK SURVEILLANCE

NOW THAT RUTH HAD MET and become friends with a black man and had also visited with two of the neighborhood boys, she was feeling almost gregarious. After a lifetime of social awkwardness and reclusive conduct, this newly acquired interest in the outside world drew her away from the insular world she and her sister had inhabited for three-quarters of a century. She spent increasingly more time sitting on her porch watching the cars and trucks go by, and checking on the comings and goings of her neighbors, especially the children. She wasn't being nosy, and she didn't gossip, so her interest was strictly in learning about a world she and Rachael had kept at bay.

"I can't believe how fast those cars and trucks go," she said to herself, as she gently propelled herself back and forth on the porch swing. "When I was a little girl it was a rutted dirt road and all we saw were buckboards and carriages. Then came the steam car we saw occasionally, then Mr. Ford's little black car, now all this. If I tried to walk across the road I'd probably get run over, and the driver wouldn't even notice. He'd think he hit a pothole and curse the road department. Where are they all going in such a hurry? I sure don't like seeing those boys out on the road. That little Blake just scampers along, crossing and re-crossing. Graham does the same thing. Those boys aren't nearly careful enough. You'd think with all the dogs and cats that get run over right here on this curve the boys would realize they could be run over, too.

"That little boy that lives on the other side of the Flournoys is going to get in trouble with the law. I may have to go have a word with his parents. I saw him standin' in the Flournoy driveway throwin' rocks at the big trailer behind the trucks going by. I heard the loud bang when the rock hit the side of the trailer. I went out on the porch and called to him, but he ran away.

"Here lately it's really been busy over there at the Flournoys. Where do all those children come from? Must be from those houses over there next to the golf course. This area's gotten crowded since the end of the war. I don't like the look of all those...slingshots. Those boys shoot at birds and squirrels and trucks and...each other! They could put out an eye doin' that. David brought down Goliath with a slingshot. I hope those boys know that story.

"Graham and that little Blake cut through my yard a lot. Always barefoot, always no shirt on. You'd never see half-naked boys in my day. That other blond friend of Graham's comes through here, too. Wish I could meet him. Tell him not to throw rocks at trucks. Find out his name. They're all handsome boys. Maybe I'll stop them one day when they're passin' through. Offer them some lemonade. Since I already know Graham and Blake, maybe they won't run off. I think Blake is the son of that nice young woman across the street who came by a while back collectin' for the March of Dimes. Mrs. Flournoy is very nice, but I've met her only a couple of times. She's got those older children that are on the go a lot, so she's busy with them. She must have a lot of energy.

"Back during the war she had those foreign soldiers comin' to her house. They played that modern music night and day. Rachael, do you remember that day two of them rang our doorbell, thinkin' they were in the right place? They looked handsome in their uniforms, and they wore their caps at a rakish angle. The one who spoke was a handsome boy. He had straight blond hair combed straight back. His hair tonic was a little strong. His smile was nice, but his teeth were a little crooked. His accent was British, so they must have been British soldiers. The other boy didn't say much, but he looked nice, too. He was a little shorter and had black, curly hair.

After we told them the Flournoys live across the road, they went down to the taxicab and paid the driver. After the taxicab left they walked across the road to the Flournoy house. I sometimes still think about those boys and wonder if they survived the war. The British people had a much worse time of it than we did.

"I know those children can play sweetly. The other day I saw those three boys on the Flournoy front porch. It looked like they were playin' jacks and havin' a great time. They did a lot of talkin' too. That Graham uses his arms a lot when he's talkin'.

"Wonder why I never see any girls. Except for the Flournoy girls I never see any. When I'm ridin' with Cousin Bea I see girls all over the place, but not around here. Those roughnecks have probably scared them off. They're probably afraid to leave the house. Might get shot at. In a few more years those boys are goin' to be very interested in those girls. Maybe I'll get Bea to drive through that new neighborhood. I bet I'll see some girls over there. I bet they're playin' with dolls, skippin' rope, playin' hopscotch...

"I'm just an old woman. The good Lord has seen fit to keep me alive, and I figure he wants more out of me than regular church attendance. I don't know what that could be, but I'll keep my eyes and ears open and maybe He'll give me a sign."

A Library Encounter

As Gayle Freemont made his way down the dirt path between the sidewalk and the eastern wing of the library, he kept his head down for two reasons. He wanted to avoid any mud puddles that might be in the path since the recent rain, and he was ashamed about having to use the Colored Entrance to the Carnegie Library of Riverton. The City Council had passed a resolution to put in a concrete sidewalk like the ones in the front of the library, but the monies hadn't yet been allocated for the project.

An imposing, granite building graced by ornate Corinthian pillars at the top of wide granite steps, the library conveyed a massiveness and sense of permanence that gave the white citizens great pride as a symbol of their devotion to Knowledge.

"Can I help you?" said the librarian assigned to the Colored Desk in the dank basement room.

"Yes, I'm Gayle Freemont. I called about checking out *An Annotated. . .*

"I've got the book right here, Gayle," she said, reaching under the counter to retrieve a slim volume of monographs on social hierarchy patterns in the South since the Civil War. She tossed it on the countertop and quickly began stamping due dates. Since his encounter with Ruth St. John, Gayle had developed an intense interest in a social system that elevates a white town drunk above a black scientist like George Washington Carver. The librarian's curt manner was perceived by Gayle as further evidence of this disparity.

But the truth of her motivation was that she was as embarrassed by her rudeness as Gayle was offended. Only twenty-two years old and newly graduated from the university, she had no experience with educated black people and felt uncomfortable dealing with them. Being newly hired she had been given an assignment that the more senior librarians avoided for the same reason. And like them she was given no instructions on how to relate to black library patrons that varied from janitors and chauffeurs to doctors, professors and highly successful businessmen.

As he left the library, still looking at the rough path, he made a mental note to himself never to come there again.

In the future he would get all of his Carnegie library books through inter-library loan at the college.

Upon reaching the city sidewalk he turned left and walked toward the southeast corner in front of the library. Just as he reached the corner and stopped to wait for the traffic light to change, a white woman with serious acne scars walked up and stood next to him. Glancing down at the book in Gayle's hand, Priscilla Andrews said,

"Looks pretty deep to me."

Gayle darted a glance at her, reflexively brought his right hand up to touch the brim of his straw hat and commented, "Uh, yes'm, I guess so" and glanced about nervously.

Keeping her gaze fixed on the side of his face, Priscilla continued, "Do you teach sociology?"

"No, ma'am," Gayle muttered as the light changed and he took off walking briskly to the other side. Sensing a chance to interact with what appeared to be a professor at the black college, Priscilla took off as quickly as Gayle did, matching him stride for stride.

"I'd be interested in knowing your view of racial integration." Gayle said nothing and walked faster. Suddenly realizing how threatened the poor man must be, accosted by a white woman, she quickly slowed down and looked around to see if anyone was watching. Seeing no one close by she gave a sigh of relief and berated herself for once again behaving recklessly.

Unlike most Riverton women, Priscilla did not feel uncomfortable talking with an educated black person because even though she was born in Riverton, she had lived in Philadelphia from the time she was three until she graduated from high school. But she was Southern enough to understand that interaction between white women and black men in the South was fraught with danger. Thinking quickly she decided to follow Gayle at a discreet distance to see if she could possibly find an opportunity to talk to him. She punctuated her resolve by tossing the hefty summer reading, Gone With the Wind, under her left arm and walking purposefully to the other side of the street.

She noted out of the corner of her eye that Gayle was walking toward the center of town, so she paused to look into a window display to give him time to extend the distance between them. Then she turned in his direction and walked leisurely down the sidewalk, occasionally pausing in front of a storefront but always making note of where the bobbing straw hat was headed. There were three other straw hats in the vicinity, but Gayle's bobbed in a distinctive way.

When he reached the town square, he turned right and stopped at the Colored Window of Floyd's diner. He ordered Floyd's Famous Meatloaf Sandwich and an RC Cola. Then he took the food across the street and sat on the bus stop bench. He began eating his food while thumbing through his book. The bench was next to the sidewalk facing the street. Behind him, on the other side of the sidewalk, was City Park, which was heavily shaded and full of daylilies, geraniums, canalilies, and other seasonal flowers. Here and there among the flowerbeds were rose bushes sporting red, yellow and white blooms. In addition to several benches scattered about the park, in the center was a gazebo where summer concerts were held. The black citizens were not allowed in the park except on concert night when they could use a specially designated section where folding chairs were set up.

Seeing him cross the street with his sandwich and drink, Priscilla suddenly realized that she was hungry and left the hardware store window display she pretended to be interested in and walked over to Floyd's to get something for herself. She took her pimento cheese and tomato sandwich and Seven-Up across to the park without even glancing at Gayle, who, engrossed in his book and sandwich, didn't notice her. She took a seat in the gazebo where she could see him and nibbled at the food while thinking intently about how to have a conversation with this man whose apparent knowledge intrigued her. As she considered several possible solutions, she marveled at how extraordinarily limited the relations between the races were.

Being a somewhat "brazen woman" with a devious mind and a strong love of adventure, Priscilla finally hit upon a plan she thought could work, although it did carry a degree of risk. But she had enough experience with middle class black people to know that she had better than a fifty-fifty chance of pulling it off. After laying down her sandwich, she reached in her purse, took out a slip of notepaper, and put it on top of her novel. She then took out her fountain pen and began writing:

"You like to study social issues and I do too. I teach fifth grade at Broad Street Elementary, and I suspect you teach at the colored college. If you would care to discuss the current racial controversy with me, I would be very pleased to meet with you. I think a very public place such as a classroom at St. Luke would make a good place to meet. My name is Priscilla Andrews and my telephone number is 42755. If I don't hear from you I will assume that you don't want to meet and I will understand why.

Priscilla Andrews"

After reading the note several times, she folded it in half and placed the novel on top of it on the bench while she finished her sandwich and drink. She dropped her trash into a nearby receptacle and strolled down the sidewalk toward Gayle, still sitting at the bus stop. Holding the note in her left hand she took a deep breath and turned toward Gayle. When she got alongside him, she quickly stooped down and pretended to pick up the note.

"I believe you dropped this from your book," she said while trying hard to appear indifferent. Handing him the note she continued down the sidewalk and out of the park area. When she got sufficiently far away she made her way back to where she had parked her car and drove home. When she had quickly glanced at his face, with its highly surprised expression, she couldn't determine if he recognized her or not. Probably not, since he barely glanced at her during the street crossing. She busied herself with various household chores while waiting for a phone call.

No call came that day or the next. She had just about decided that he would not call when, early one evening, the phone rang, and a tremulous voice said,

"Mrs. Andrews?"

"Miss"

"This...this is Gayle Freemont, the colored man you gave the note to at the bus stop."

169

"I'm so glad you called, Mr. Freemont. I want to talk to you about your views on racial integration, but I know the difficulties of having such a conversation between a white woman and a colored man in the South." Gayle was smart enough to know that some extremist group, maybe the Klan, might be setting him up to see if he would step over the line.

"Is there some kind of work you need for me to do, ma'am?"

"No, it's as I say. I want to talk to you. Look, I'm a teacher. I was born in the South, but I spent all my growing up years in Philadelphia. There's nothing nefarious about my request. I'm interested, concerned about the racial problem and want to get the point of view of an educated colored man."

Gayle reflected on her words for a few seconds then said, "Your suggestion that we meet at my college is a good one. I, too, am eager to discuss this issue with an educated white person. What I propose is this: you bring a male colleague, and I will bring a colored female colleague. We'll meet in the faculty conference room, and if anybody asks what we're doing, we could tell them we're an ad hoc committee formed to study the school lunch program as it applies to the colored schools. Everybody knows of Superintendent Flournoy's interest in this."

They agreed to contact their respective colleagues and get back in touch with each other in a day or two. Gayle gave her his number before they hung up. Priscilla decided to ask her principal, Reynolds Foster, and after a little hesitation and a few questions he agreed to come with her. Gayle was able to recruit Justina Holliday, one of his colleagues in the earth sciences department. Raised and educated in the Boston area, Justina had a strong intellectual and personal interest in race relations.

On the day of the meeting, Priscilla and Reynolds drove to St. Luke in Reynolds' '39 Buick. They passed between the red brick columns of the main gate and parked in front of the squat, undistinguished brick administration building. Since the college was between terms, there were few students, staff and faculty on campus, so the two white people drew little attention. They were directed to the dark, wood-paneled conference room where Gayle stood as they entered the room. When he extended his hand to Reynolds, the older man hesitated momentarily and then took his hand in a warm shake. His hesitation was due to his inability to recall ever shaking a black man's hand. Gayle introduced Justina and nodded to Priscilla. He then sat quietly waiting for one of the two white people to initiate the conversation. Finally, after a few uncomfortable seconds, both Reynolds and Priscilla started talking at once, stopped, laughed, then invited the other to start. Laughing again, Priscilla quickly took the initiative and asked,

"What is the feeling in the colored community about the integration talk?"

Gayle replied, "Among the faculty members here there is a lot of talk about it. Many in administration, especially the old ones, don't much like the talk because they are afraid of repercussions and seem to have the opinion that it is better not to endanger the college with such talk, that integration will come in time. But the faculty, especially the young ones—-and one notable old philosophy prof—-are very much interested in talking about it, not only among themselves but also with their students."

Justina added, "I'm one of those who likes to talk about it with my colleagues, but I'm very careful about bringing it up with students. For one thing, the topic of racial integration is hard to work into a course which deals with tectonic plates, seismology, continental drift, and the like. But my main reason for avoiding it is fear. I heard so many stories about the South growing up in Boston that I'm afraid."

"You know, we whites in the South have the same problem," replied Reynolds. "We have many misconceptions about colored people because of our limited contact. We see only the lowest levels of colored society and think those represent all colored people. My first contact with a colored person who spoke proper English was Louis Johnson, a first lieutenant from Hartford, Connecticut. I served with him in

Europe during the war. But I'm not so sure the Northerners are much better off. I saw a lot of racial prejudice in Rhode Island and New York while I was in the service."

"What we seem to be saying, then," offered Priscilla, "is that we need some way for the two races to get to know each other better. How do we do that?" This last question engaged the foursome for the rest of the hour-long meeting, but they came up with no solid suggestions. They parted company with the promise to continue working on a solution and to keep in touch with each other.

As she and Reynolds drove through the gates of the college on their way out, Priscilla reflected on how complex the issue was and how it may never be worked out in her lifetime.

THE GARLIC MYSTERY

"HEY, BLAKE! WAIT ON ME!" yelled Graham as he ran along his gravel driveway and crossed the highway into Ruth's yard. "Where you goin'!? We gotta work on some plans for the battle!"

"I'm headin' over behind Miss Ruth's house to pick some garlic."

"Some what?"

"Some garlic. Mr. Henry told me to bring him some more garlic and anything else that looks interesting I can find. Mr. Henry told me to ask Miz Ruth if it would be okay."

"How is it when the Renegades are gettin' ready to invade us with a bunch of older boys and a mawk orange cannon you are thinkin' about garlic?"

"I found some stinky weed behind her house when I was cuttin' through from Thurman Road, and when I wuz walkin' down our driveway I saw Mr. Henry workin' in his garden. I went over and showed him the stinky weed, and he told me it wuz garlic."

Roland and Charlotte Henry were a retired couple who lived next door to the Armisteads, on the west side. A history buff, Roland Henry knew, when Blake told him that he had found it close to some pieces of old planking and bricks, that such garlic probably came from a plot planted by slaves, and it just came back up every spring since then.

"Good morning, boys," Ruth said through a half-open door, her voice revealing surprise to see Blake and Graham standing there.

"Good morning, Miz Ruth," said Blake, peering into a dark foyer. "Mr. Henry wohnts to know if there wuz some slave cabins behind your house durin' the War Between the States."

"Well, if you'll tell me your names, I'll tell you what I know. Won't you come in?" Ruth led the boys back to the kitchen and sat them at the kitchen table. Both boys accepted a glass of ice tea then Ruth sat down with them.

"Now, tell me about yourselves." As she asked the question, Ruth surprised herself how sociable she had become. She would never have been so friendly when Rachael was alive.

"I'm Blake Armistead, ma'am. I live across the road next to the Henrys."

"I'm Graham Flournoy, ma'am. I live directly across the road."

"I know your father and mother, Graham. They were so kind when my sister Rachael died last winter. Your father was over here a while back helping me get a snake that was loose here in the kitchen." Both boys instinctively jerked their feet off the floor at the mention of the snake.

"To what do I owe the pleasure of this visit, boys?" she said, but then remembered the question Blake had asked. "Oh, the slave quarter. Yes, my grandfather, Rem Aldrich, who built this house, had slaves. They lived in some cabins down the hill a ways behind the house. The cabins have been gone for many, many years." A short silence followed while everyone took a sip of tea. Then Blake said,

"I wuz walkin' through your back field the other day and I saw some stinkweeds. I took some and showed them to Mr. Henry. He said they wuz garlic. He said slaves probably planted it."

"He's right. I remember when I was a little girl playing down there in the field. I saw that garlic close by lots of old planks and bricks, a few bottles, tin cups, and the like. I asked my mama about it, and she said that when <u>she</u> was a little girl there had been a slave quarter there, and the slaves maintained what was called The Patch, a vegetable garden that supplied everybody on the plantation.

"Did your mama see any Yankees?" asked Graham.

"No, but their armies passed close by. They destroyed a textile mill a few miles from here on the river. Would you like a tea cake?"

"Yes, thank you," both boys said simultaneously. Ruth got up from the table and took three cookies from the cookie jar next to the breadbasket on the kitchen counter. As she placed the cookie plate on the table, Graham reached for a cookie, asking as he did,

"Miz Ruth, why can't the colored people go to white restaurants or picture shows, and why do they have to sit on the back of the bus?"

Ruth looked slightly uncomfortable as she contemplated his question. Graham waited expectantly, as he gingerly bit down on his cookie. Blake stared at the cookie in his hand as though he had never seen one before.

"Well, Graham, it's kinda hard to explain. I guess you boys know--well, maybe you don't--that the colored people were brought here from Africa as slaves, and — "

"The colored people in Africa are called natives in the Tarzan movies," interjected Blake. "They are always carryin' bundles on their head and don't wear nothin' but a piece of cloth in front and back."

"It's not polite to interrupt, Blake."

"I'm sorry."

"As I was saying, the slaves were brought over from Africa. They were brought to do the work on the plantations. After a while there was talk about setting them free because some believed it's not right to hold anyone in bondage."

"Is that the same thing as holding them as slaves?" asked Blake.

"Yes, exactly. The talk was mostly coming from the North where the white people didn't need slave labor. My grandfather and the other growers at the time depended heavily on their slaves, so there was an impasse--big disagreement--about this, which eventually led to war. The North won the war and they imposed some terrible burdens on the South. One of these was to set all the slaves free and let them be citizens the same as the white folks. My mama told me that when freedom came, some of our slaves left and headed north, but most of them stayed with our family and became sharecroppers. My Granddaddy Richard worked with several colored sharecroppers at the end of the last century. The Yankees put colored men in government posts and all sorts of other things, which was addin' insult to injury. After twenty years or so of this, the white people got control again and decided it would be best if white and colored were separated. For as long as I can remember there have been colored schools, colored restaurants, colored theaters, and whenever there have been no separate facilities there have been separate accommodations, such as colored water fountains next to white ones, colored restrooms close to the white ones."

Ruth abruptly stopped her monologue when she saw that Blake was just looking at different spots in the room, oblivious to what she was saying. Graham kept his eyes on her, but his brow was getting increasingly more furrowed.

"What I mean to say, boys, is that keeping the races separated seems to work just fine. Everybody seems to be happy with the arrangement. You don't hear any complaining about it from anybody." But even as she said this, she knew it wasn't true. She knew that the black people had far less than the whites and probably did complain. In fact, Germaine had made a couple of subtle remarks that indicated as much. And then of course there was the matter of Gayle Freemont.

"Why don't you boys just run on down there to the garlic patch and see what you can find for Mr. Henry."

A Rainy Afternoon on the Screened Porch

After calling Todd and Blake, Graham called Ralph, who had agreed to come over for a game of Monopoly. Graham had hoped the rainy weather would be over by lunchtime, but the overcast sky promised an afternoon of steady rain and occasional cloudbursts. That morning he had enjoyed playing in the rain with Todd and Blake. They raced sticks in the water rushing through the ditch in front of the Flournoy house, and they threw mud balls at each other in a running battle through the field behind the Flournoy "back field." When a thunderstorm erupted and lightning began to flash, Anna yelled for the boys to get in the house. The crashing thunder indicated the lightning was close, so she felt better when all three boys were cleaning up and drying off on the back porch. Todd and Blake then ran home to have lunch and get dry clothes.

Still feeling a little cold from their morning escapades, and knowing the screened porch would be cool, all three boys wore a tee shirt and a long sleeve cotton shirt. Todd brought his own, but Blake had to borrow one from Graham. Since he hadn't got wet, Ralph just wore a Superman tee shirt. They set up the card table and folding chairs in the center of the porch. Graham placed the Monopoly game box on the wicker coffee table in front of the wicker settee.

"I'm the cannon!" yelled Blake.

"I'm the racecar!" cried Ralph.

"I'm the battleship!" yelled Todd. "You can be the iron, Gray ham."

"I'm the cowboy, Todd-Clod."

Soon the board was open on the card table and all of the player pieces, dice, cards, hotels and houses were spilled across the board. All four boys quickly put them in their proper places. While giving each player some play money, Graham made note of an occasional chip in the wood of the green houses and red hotels. He wondered if they could get replacement pieces.

"High roll goes first!" cried Blake, as he snatched up the dice and began shaking them vigorously. He believed that the longer and stronger you shook the dice the higher the roll would be. Just before the other boys yelled at him, Blake dramatically tossed the dice onto the center of the board. Despite Blake's effort, he got only a three. Todd got the highest roll and moved his piece to St. Charles Place.

"I'll buy that!" announced Todd, who quickly drew out a hundred dollar bill and two twenties from under his side of the board. While Graham fished for the deed in the deed pack, Ralph grabbed the dice and rolled a seven.

"Chance!" Ralph shouted. He drove his racecar to the spot and took the top orange card. After reading it, he tried to stick it on the bottom of the stack, but Todd grabbed his hand, snatched the card away, and read aloud:

"Go directly to Jail! Do not pass Go! Do not collect $200!" Todd then grabbed Ralph's racecar and stuck it in the jail.

"Don't worry Ralph-y! Your sweetheart, Camille, will get you out!" teased Blake.

"She <u>aint</u> my sweetheart, Blake-eee! She makes me throw up!"

"Janie said you wuz talking to her in Woolworth's yesterday."

"Your fat sister is stupid! I wuz in there with Mama, and she came over and asked me if I liked Rosie Birch. I told her I wouldn't like Rosie Birch if she wuz the only person in the world!"

"Roll the dice, Graham!" ordered Todd, who had grown

tired of the bickering. Graham landed on Oriental Avenue and when he saw that Blake was hurrying to roll the dice, he shouted, "I'll buy that!" and pulled out a hundred for the bank and flipped through the cards for his deed. Now that it was his turn, Blake didn't take so long shaking the dice, and it came up double fours.

"Doubles means I get to roll again!" Blake announced as he moved his cannon down the board to Vermont Avenue, which he bought. He then rolled a three and a one and moved to the Electric Company, but didn't want to buy it. When Ralph didn't roll doubles on his next throw, which would have got him out of jail free, he started to pay his $50 but then saw that his eight would put him on Luxury Tax, so he decided to wait until his next turn.

The boys continued taking turns, with few interruptions, until all the property had been bought and they were quarreling about how to purchase houses and hotels.

"You boys sound like you could use some strawberry Kool-Aid and vanilla wafers," Anna said, as she walked onto the porch and set a tray down on the other end of the wicker coffee table.

While sipping their Kool-Aid and nibbling on their cookies, the boys teased Ralph about Camille and Rosie. Then Ralph counter-attacked.

"Graham likes Gay-lene."

"I do not! I mean...I don't like her the way you mean. She's much older than me! She's like an older sister!"

"So, your sister is a nigger?" asked Ralph.

"No! She's <u>like</u> a sister!"

"And she <u>aint no nigger!</u>" shouted Ruthelle, who walked onto the porch shaking a feather duster at Ralph. All four boys, embarrassed, immediately shut up and looked down at the board.

"Ralph Butler, I'm ashamed of you! You've known Gaylene since you wuz a little boy and now you talkin' like that. I oughta call yo' mama and tell her how you talk! No, Gaylene aint Graham's sister, but she helped raise him! Gaylene is a <u>colored</u> girl, and she will soon become a <u>colored</u> woman when she gets married. I want all you boys to watch yo' mouth! If you don't I'm goan get my Octagon Soap and wash <u>out</u> yo' mouth! Now git on 'bout yo' bidness!" she ordered as she spun on her heel and got back to her dusting in the living room.

After she left, the boys sat listening to the soft but steady rain bounce off the roof of the screened porch. In one form or another all four of them wondered why saying "nigger" was okay for some adults but not for others. Graham also wondered why there was such a strong separation of the races. He loved Ruthelle and wanted the best for her, but he knew that she and Gaylene would never have the best of anything because of their race. And he realized that his mother would never have to explain to anyone that her children are white people.

He heaved a sigh and reminded himself that soon he will be in charge of defending the tree house fort from Murray's mock orange cannon.

"You think we need more men for the battle?" asked Graham, as he picked up the dice and began shaking them.

"Who you goan get? The National Guard?" said Todd. "We got just about every boy around here. Me and Ralph are gittin' deadly with our grenades. Murray aint gonna know what hit him."

"How many men did Murray bring last year?" asked Blake.

"It wad'n more'n four or five, was it Graham?" asked Todd.

"That sounds about right. But I remember they were awfully good," said Graham, as he moved his piece along the board. "I hope you're right about the grenades. That could give us the edge."

"You landed on Kentucky Avenue, Gray ham!" shouted Blake. "I own all three red, so your rent is two times $18 or [multiplies 18 times 2 with his finger on the table top] $36!

THE WEDDING DRESS

"MISTER FLOURNOY, CAN I SPEAK to you for a minute?" said Ruthelle, slowly walking into Pete's study and closing the door behind her.

"Of course you can, Ruthelle," said Pete, as he lay his fountain pen down on the ink blotter and looked up.

"I understand what you told me about the separation of the races and how we can't share certain things like clothes," she said, standing directly in front of his big mahogany desk in her starched, light blue uniform and white apron, her hands folded demurely in front.

"The problem is with Gaylene. She don't understand. She's spent most of her life in this house and knows every inch of it. She knows that furnace and coal bin in the basement where her and Maxine wuz playin', and Maxine got so black they looked like twins. She knows that big, scary attic above this room. She knows that upstairs back porch where her and your children sunbathed. It didn't bother her one bit that she was already dark enough.

"To her, she is a daughter and a sister to this family. Maybe it was wrong of me to bring her with me so much, but I didn't know what else to do when my man ran off and left us. I coulda used my mama to babysit, but she's off there in Mississippi. And old Aunt Minnie next door. She watched Gaylene a few times, but that old woman drinks cheap wine all day long, and I just did'n feel right about it.

"I haven't told that child what you said. It would break her heart. She understands the separation of the races. She sees it every day. But she dud'n see this family as bein' white, if you know what I mean."

Pete, embarrassed by her comments and ashamed, had kept his head down while she spoke. When she paused, he raised his head, and she could see his face had reddened. "What if we bought her a dress of her own?"

"That won't do no good, Mr. Flournoy. She thinks you love her as much as your own children and would want her to wear the dress same as Maxine and Susan. I been puttin' her off about the dress, but I gotta tell her sooner or later."

Pete looked back down at the ink blotter and moved the fountain pen first here then there as he reflected on what she had said. Finally he spoke. "Tell Gaylene that of course she can wear the dress. She's right. She <u>is</u> a member of this family, just as you are. If the white people get upset and the colored people get shocked...I guess that's just the way it'll have to be. As I'm sure you understand, Ruthelle, my job as county superintendent is politically sensitive. That is to say, I have to make the county commissioners happy, the mayor of Riverton happy, the governor happy, and so on. And they don't like mixin' the races. But I think this is the right thing to do, and we'll just have to hope for the best. I like to think that I put moral and ethical considerations above all others in my decision makin' as superintendent, but I'm sure I haven't from time to time. This decision may not be the right one politically...but it <u>is</u> the right one in the eyes of God." Pete then regretted giving a speech. He decided he was too inclined to speechify and must resist sounding like a politician. But the oratory didn't bother Ruthelle.

Breaking into a big smile, Ruthelle hugged herself and said, "Thank you! Thank you so much! That takes a big weight off my heart...God bless you, Mr. F!" Ruthelle turned and left his office with a much lighter step than when she entered. Pete put his elbows on the ink blotter and his head in his hands. As he stared at the blank, green paper, he noticed, out of the corner of his eye, that the fountain pen was leaking, and a black ink spot was spreading on the clean, green blotter.

BREAKING THE NEWS TO BOB

JANE FORRESTER WAS PLAGUED BY guilt. The quaint houses and shops on the island had charmed and diverted her for a while, and she found the Canadian people to be very friendly, but she felt she <u>had</u> to do something to let her mother know she was okay. After pondering her dilemma for a while she devised a plan for getting a message not only to her mother and brother but also to Bob and some friends. She would write the letters and send them in a manila envelope from Halifax to the widowed husband of a friend in Miami. Becky Rouse had been a sorority sister at Flo Hennessy, and they had stayed in touch over the years, but Becky had died of breast cancer two years before. Frank Rouse would be content just to mail the letters without needing elaborate explanations. Jane would make up some kind of plausible story as to why she wants her family to think she is in Miami, and Frank would be content with that.

Bob had paid no attention to Jane's old friends, so there was little chance he would connect Becky to the letter he would receive, and since Jane had taken all of her address books, even the Christmas card book, there should be no evidence of Jane's connection to anybody in Miami. She believed he would assume she mailed the letters herself since she had planted the idea of a Caribbean escape, and had even left a phony note to herself to inquire about flights out of Miami.

The reason for Jane's extreme secrecy was the threat Bob posed. In her mind he was not only cruel, selfish, and vindictive, but also used a web of contacts to get what he wanted. He had connections at all levels of government, all the way to Washington, and he had "business associates" among the bosses in the Phenix City, Alabama mob that controlled gambling and prostitution. In 1947, Phenix City was "sin city" for thousands of soldiers stationed at Ft. Benning across the state line in Georgia.

All these connections were not as solid as Jane believed they were, and Bob was not as dangerous as she thought he was, but in her mind he would do anything to get revenge.

Dear Mama,

I feel rotten about leaving you and Cullen with no explanation. I suppose Bob called you. I hope he wasn't too hateful. I just couldn't take it anymore. I was in Dr. Cooper's office when I got this powerful urge to scream and cry, so I just got up and left. I decided that I wasn't going to spend any more time with that son of a bitch. But you know how dangerous he is, and how vindictive, so I had to cover my tracks carefully. I can't say any more because I don't want to put you and Cullen in danger. Just know that I'm fine, and I love you both. I'm sending Bob a letter also. If he wants to know if you got one, too, just show him this letter, which should prove to him that you know nothing about my whereabouts. I'm happy where I am, so don't worry about me.

Love, Jane

Dear Bob,

I can't tell you how good it is to be rid of you at last. You made my life a hell on earth for twenty years, but now I live in paradise. All that can spoil my life now is Mother Nature, a hurricane perhaps. Or maybe I'll contract cancer. But I would prefer to live with cancer than to live with you. With physical cancer I've always got a chance to survive through surgery or medicine, or maybe even a miraculous cure. But my cancerous relationship with you was more virulent. You abused my body with your sick sexual practices. Your humiliation of me in front of friends and relatives wore me down mentally and spiritually. Initially I stayed with you through all of that because I was a proper Southern woman and had the misguided notion that the wife must keep the marriage together at all costs. Later I stayed married to you because I was afraid of what you would do if I filed for divorce.

I don't know what you told your friends and business contacts about my disappearance, but whatever it was I'm setting the record straight by writing to my contacts and telling them the truth. I'm going to tell them what a rotten son of a bitch you are. I'm going to tell them that I have been starved for love from a real man and I have found a young, bronze god to live with me. I bought him a tuxedo on a lark, and he looks very handsome wearing your cufflinks and stickpin. I'm afraid I may have lost one of your cufflinks. The other night when we came back from a night on the town, he started kissing me on the back of the neck, a very sensual spot that you never knew about. I got so hot that I turned around and began tearing at his clothes. I think that's when I lost the cufflink. But it was well worth it, believe me.

Well, I guess that's about it. I hope your life is as miserable as mine is satisfying. I'll look forward to your death--painful I hope--so I can re-connect to my family and friends.

Jane (he Tarzan)

General Delivery
Miami, Florida

Dear Jane,

I don't understand what I have done to make you hate me so. We had our differences from time to time, but I feel we had a good marriage overall. I admit I could be bossy at times, but a man is supposed to be the king in his own castle. The pressures of my work often made me irritable, and I apologize for any cruel things I might have said.

Now that I know how you feel, I want to make amends and make a fresh start. I know we can patch up our differences and have a good life together. I'm looking at retirement in a few more years, and when that happens we can travel a lot more and really enjoy life.

I talked to your mother a while back, and she doesn't sound well. Your disappearance has hurt her deeply. At her age it's no telling what might happen to her. I think that if she saw us back together again enjoying life she would become a new woman. For her sake if not for mine, please come home.

Love,

Bob

THE SPIDER AND THE BEAR

THE BATTLE WAS ONLY A few hours away. Graham had done everything he could think of to get ready. He had rehearsed Raider strategy over and over in his head until he was certain of what they planned to do, but he was still unsure of how well their plan would work. Even though it was almost dark and close to his bedtime, he sneaked out of the house while his parents were listening to the radio. He walked into the back field and climbed up into the tree house. He lay on his stomach and looked off to the west at the setting sun, now only a sliver on the horizon. Above it were red clouds, which promised nice weather for battle day. As he contemplated the gradual transition to darkness, he sensed a transition in his life. He sensed that in some way his childhood was setting also, that when he awoke the next day he would be a different boy.

Both Daddy and Ruthelle said it's important to have confidence in yourself. I'm trying hard as I can to believe in myself, but it's hard. I wish Harold wuz home so I could ask him what he would do . . . I wish I wuz more like Todd. He always seems so sure of himself. Maybe he should be leadin' the Raiders instead of me. But all the boys look to me as their leader. Is it only because I'm a little older than Todd? Maybe it's because I don't act so quick like he does. And Todd wants me to lead, just like the others. When we have our talks, Todd always accepts what I decide we should do. But we use a lot of his ideas, too.

Pete had recently given Graham a children's book about Robert the Bruce, in the hope that the story about the king and the spider would boost his confidence. Graham read about the six battles the Scottish king lost to the English. He noted how, one rainy day, while hiding in a mountain cave, Bruce was completely despondent and was prepared to go into exile. While staring out at the dismal weather, the king observed a spider attempting to string a strand of web from one side of the cave opening to the other. After failing six times, it succeeded on the seventh try. This inspired Bruce to try one more time, and that time he drove the English back to England.

One evening when Graham sat down on the front steps with his father to discuss the story the first question he asked was, "Will we have to lose to the Renegades six times before we can win?"

"No, what that story illus...tells us is that the king and his army had the ability to win all along, but didn't try hard enough before. The king didn't get any more soldiers. He didn't get any strategic advantage in that seventh battle. The only difference was that he believed in his army. He knew they could win. He had complete confidence in the rightness of their cause and their ability to fight."

"Do we have rightness of our cause, Daddy?"

"Well, yeah, you do. This neighborhood is sort of like Scotland, and the Renegades are like the English army. You told me that the Raiders lost last year, and that should be enough. You now know the strengths and weaknesses of the Renegades.

"Ruthelle said if we don't win God has other things he wants to use us for."

"Did you discuss the battle with Ruthelle?"

"No, I know how women get about fightin'.' I just told her we wuz gonna be in a shootin' match. She told me about the same thing you did. She said I've got to believe in myself. She even told me to go up to my room and clear out a place for the trophy I'm goan win."

"Heh, heh. Ruthelle is right. Clear out that space. Imagine a big trophy standing there. Just imagining a desired outcome can oftentimes help make it happen. It all comes back to self-confidence." Pete and Graham then sat quietly for a while listening to the night sounds, smelling the gardenia, and looking at the sky.

"Isn't that the Big Dipper over there, Daddy?" asked Graham, pointing to his left.

"Yes...also known as Ursa Major, or Great Bear."

"It sure doesn't look like a bear."

"To the ancients it did. Maybe they didn't have a dipper to compare it to...Maybe the Raiders are like that group of stars. The Renegades see only a Big Dipper, but you're going to show them a Great Bear."

As he recalled that evening with his father, Graham sat up in the tree house and nervously pulled at his left ear. The last remnants of the sunset had disappeared, and the warm, humid darkness felt like black velvet on his skin. To relieve the sense of oppression Graham drew in a deep breath of night air heavily scented by the honeysuckle vines covering the fence on the west side of the field. The sweet smell reminded him of his mother, which made him feel better. He scanned the sky above the tree house until he found the Big Dipper. *We will be the Great Bear tomorrow.* Then, in the faint starlight, he searched for a spider that might be spinning its web.

BATTLE DAY AT LAST

ON THE DAY OF THE battle, the Renegades worried about the Raiders. Murray, Sam, Butch and Carl checked the two slingshots each had, to make sure they were in perfect working order. They loaded up their pockets with chinaberries, and put a bucketful into the wheelbarrow that Butch had brought from home. They planned to stop halfway to the battlefield at a small grove of mock orange trees and fill the wheelbarrow with mock oranges. Murray, Sam and Carl would roll the cannon and Butch would follow behind with the wheelbarrow. While preparing the cannon for the battle, the boys had devised a way to use a length of rebar to anchor it, to make it more stable. They had thought the 2X4 base would keep it steady, but it hadn't. The rebar this year should do the trick.

At the last meeting before "debarkation," Murray barked

his orders, "Sam, you and Carl cover me and Butch while we set up the cannon in front of their tree house! Once we get this baby anchored," he said, as he gently patted it on the frame, "it'll be all over for the rats! I figure they'll be cryin' and runnin' home to mama after I've fired about two rounds! After I'm set up, y'all set up a perimeter around me and keep the enemy pinned down while I blast their crappy house out of the tree! They're probably puttin' up extra fortifications right now, but it ain't gonna do no good!"

Following these last minute instructions and pep talk, the four boys set out down back roads and over fields on the one-mile journey to the Flournoy back field. A more motley crew would be hard to imagine. They had tied strips of cloth around their heads, and Carl had put a turkey feather in his headband. They were all shirtless, although Sara Austin did not permit Murray to leave the house without at least a T-shirt on. They all wore short pants with an elastic waistband, except for Murray, who had somewhat dressier pants with belt loops and a belt. All were barefoot except Murray, who had on his black Keds with no socks. Sam had brought a few cans of old paint from his house, so they all had painted stripes of different colors on their faces and torsos. The men who saw them on their trek were either amused or jealous. The women who saw them wondered if their mothers knew what they were up to. Fortunately for the boys, none of the adults knew who they were.

In their last few war councils the Raiders had decided to lure the cannon as they had planned. They figured that Murray was so cocksure of Renegade superiority that he wouldn't be suspicious of anything. So they carried through on the plan to guide them to the exact spot where they wanted them, directly in front of the fort. Mister, Lonnie and Blake would be in the mulberry tree off to their left, drawing their fire. Ralph and Todd would be lying down on top of the chicken house off to their right, with a nice supply of mud grenades and a book of matches. Graham would be shooting from the tree house in front of them to make sure he had Murray's complete attention. With the Renegades' attention drawn to the tree house and their left flank, the mud grenade team would be able to rain down grenades and take them completely by surprise. Ralph and Todd had practiced enough from the chicken house, with both live and dead grenades, to know exactly how much of an arc was needed for the burning fuse to contact the powder and detonate at the right moment. They refined their technique, with Ralph lighting and Todd throwing, so that almost all of the blasts were between ten and fifteen feet above the ground. Ten feet was ideal because it would be about five feet over their heads, which would give a nice, wide pattern of fragments with enough power to sting them good.

The Raiders dressed up in their "battle gear" also. Mister wore a loin cloth over his underpants, in the style of Tarzan. He carried his chinaberries in a canvas bag tied to his waist and hanging at his side.

Blake and Lonnie wore tee shirts and broken off small mulberry limbs to stick in the sleeves, collar, pants legs, and belt, in an effort to camouflage themselves. All three boys smeared themselves with wine-colored mulberry juice. On the chicken house, Todd and Ralph had to be especially free in their movements, so they had on nothing except their short pants. A privet bush grew on the front side of the chicken house and some of its limbs extended over the edge of the corrugated tin roof. The boys would slide down into the hedge at the roof's edge where they couldn't be seen and where it would be cooler once the sun heated up the roof.

The morning of battle day was sunny and clear. The early morning dew was burned off by nine o'clock and the temperature was already in the eighties. By nine-thirty the Raiders had completed their final war council in the tree house and were getting their supplies together and checking out their battle stations and tactics.

"Don't be lookin' to see if the grenade goes off!" said Todd. "Just watch me. When you see me reachin' for another grenade you strike your match and protect it from the wind. When I jerk my throwin' arm back like this, you light the fuse about halfway up like I showed you. That way the fuse'll stay lit and go off at just the right time." Ralph just nodded mutely at his instructions.

Up in the tree house, Graham and Lonnie were making preparations to receive fire from the cannon. It had been decided at the last council that maybe Lonnie should be with Graham since Lonnie was the least experienced of the Raiders. He didn't much like being shot at with those lethal mock oranges, but he felt good about being with Graham.

"Let's throw the mattress over the sawhorse now," said Graham, so he and Lonnie each grabbed a loop on the side and hoisted it over the modified sawhorse. They had already nailed the legs of the sawhorse to the floor of the tree house, and now he and Lonnie set about nailing the ends of the mattress to the floor as well. The effect was a tent made out of mattress material that they could either get behind or inside of to protect themselves.

Graham and Todd had found the double bed mattress out on the street in front of a house down River Road toward Meader's Creek. While walking along Graham had been pondering a good defense against the cannon, so when he saw the discarded mattress he had an epiphany. Getting it home had been a very big job, but he felt it had been well worth it, now that it was installed.

"You stay inside and shoot out the left side. I'll stay behind and shoot over the top. Be sure to make lots of noise so we can keep Murray's attention focused on us."

Blake and Mister had already made their plans, and Mister was climbing a tree at the edge of the golf course to look out for the Renegades. Blake was comfortably seated in the main fork of the mulberry tree eating mulberries. After the Raiders had waited for a half an hour they were getting thirsty, and Blake was just about to jump down and run to the spigot in the Flournoy yard when a shout went up from Mister

"Here they come!! They're comin' along the fairway next to the McGregor house! I think they're headed for the wahter fountain next to that tee box!" he shouted with envy, since he too was thirsty. All of the boys knew exactly where the McGregor country estate was on the eastern side of the golf course and about how long it would take the Renegades to reach them.

THE RENEGADES ADVANCE

"DON'T DRINK ALL THE WAHTER, Murray. We're thirsty, too," said Carl.

"A wahter fountain dud'n go empty, dummy," said Murray as he stepped away from the fountain wiping his mouth with the back of his hand.

Each of the other boys got two or three swallows of water before getting pushed aside by another boy. Soon the thirst of the Renegades had been slaked, and they stood in a circle discussing the last leg of their advance.

"Do you think they know we're almost there, Murray?" asked Carl.

"Yeah. I expect the little sissies have been up since daybreak bitin' their nails and lookin' out for us. Butch, you be the scout and run ahead to see what they're doin'. Carl can roll the wheelbarrow."

Butch ran over to the right edge of the golf course and ran in a crouch in the tall grass in the heavy rough. The rest of the boys moved steadily along in the fairway so that the cannon would roll easily.

Looking through his "spyglass," a cardboard tube from a toilet paper roll, Mister could see Butch bobbing up and down in the tall grass and, farther along, in the fairway, the other boys moving the cannon and wheelbarrow steadily toward him.

"What do you see, Mister?" said Graham, who had come to the bottom of Mister's tree.

"I see 'em comin' along the fairway. I think that's Butch I see sneakin' along in the tall grass."

"I gotta get back to my battle station. You let out two short whistles if they turn in where we want them to. If they go past that spot, let out one long whistle. I'll let the others know if they come in further down."

Graham had just got settled back behind the mattress in the treehouse when he heard the two sharp, short whistles. This meant that no instructions would need to be passed on, so he pushed a small handful of chinaberries into his mouth. He noticed immediately that their taste was more bitter than usual and realized it was because his mouth had gone dry. He rolled the berries around in his mouth to stimulate a saliva flow and ignored the bitterness.

The Renegades had heard the whistles, too, and paused to look up in Mister's direction, but he had pressed himself against the trunk of the tree deep in the canopy and couldn't be seen. After a few seconds Murray ordered them to advance through the generous opening in the fence and to follow the surprisingly clear and smooth pathway just inside the Flournoy property.

Soon after they started moving again, Mister was out of his lookout tree and running wide open for the mulberry tree, where Blake waited, eyes wide open and mouth stained purple.

"They're comin' along the path just as we planned!" Mister said breathlessly to Blake as he scampered up the tree to his station a few feet away from Blake.

Graham saw Mister climbing the tree and turned to face the chicken house. He spit a berry into the pouch of his slingshot and shot down at the tin roof. The sharp clang of berry hitting tin was Todd's cue to get ready, so he and Ralph waddled out from the bush duck-fashion until they could just see over the peak of the roofline. The target area they had practiced hitting was clearly visible. To help insure that Murray brought the cannon exactly to that spot rather than someplace else, they had cleared out a circular area some twenty feet in diameter and hoped it wouldn't be too obvious.

"I can't believe we are makin' such easy time with the cannon," said Murray just as Butch arrived back from his reconnaissance of the battle field, chewing on wild plums he had stumbled on.

"Looks like they're in the fort," mumbled Butch, who then cleared his mouth by spitting a plum stone at Carl. "They got some kind of doohicky up there that looks like a tent."

"A tent!?" exclaimed Murray. "That ain't goan stop nothin'! Sam, you and Carl come in from both sides and get 'em in a crossfire! Butch, you stay close and cover me!"

The Battle Is Joined

As the two other boys scurried off in a crouch to take up positions on opposite sides of the treehouse, Butch and Murray quickly rolled the cannon into a strategic position some fifty feet in front of the tree. Murray didn't see the clearing that Todd and Ralph had prepared for him, but he did stop close to that spot. Sam was partially hidden in the tall pasture grass, and Carl was positioned behind a stump and a pokeberry bush. Murray wondered why they were holding their fire as he and Butch set up the cannon with the rebar brace driven in the ground.

When Butch handed Murray a mock orange for the first shot, Graham yelled "Fire!" and a chinaberry fusillade pelted the Renegades. Sam was hit from behind by one shot from Blake and two from Mister before he realized where they were and vigorously rubbed the welts on his neck and back. Carl got off a shot up at the mattress, having nothing else to shoot at. Graham and Lonnie retaliated by quickly stepping out from the mattress and shooting down at him. One of their berries struck the stump, the other a nearby honeysuckle clump.

Meanwhile, Butch shot up into the tree while Murray drew back the inner tube to launch the one-pound mock orange. Just as he was about to release it, he heard a high-pitched whistling sound, "wheeeeeeee!" coming from his right, followed by a shattering blast in front of the cannon. "Ka-blam!" The blast startled him and he flinched in his release, causing the mock orange to sail over the mattress, strike a limb, and split in two, both halves tumbling harmlessly to the ground.

"What was that!!?" yelled Butch.

"They got mortars!!" yelled Murray. At that moment, they again heard off to their right, "wheeeeeeeee!" followed by another explosion, a little closer this time, which pelted them with mud and sand. Todd's imitation of an incoming mortar shell was eerily effective.

Meanwhile, Sam was pinned down by Blake and Mister in a firefight, as was Carl with Graham and Lonnie. Unsure what to do next, Murray quickly decided to go after the mortar, so he jerked the rebar out of the ground and instructed Butch to turn the cannon in the direction of the chicken house. While grabbing a mock orange out of the wagon, he heard the whistling sound and quickly turned his back to it just as a third explosion sprayed him and Butch. As Butch drove the rebar into the ground Murray drew back the mock orange, taking aim through the gunpowder smoke at the two figures he saw on the roof of the chicken house. Todd and Ralph had a bad fuse and were quickly working with a substitute grenade when a tremendous ka-whump! sounded from the upslope of the tin roof in front of them, followed by a whizzing sound as the mock orange ricocheted off the roof and flew over their heads. They instinctively dropped to the hot roof but quickly jumped up into a squat when the metal burned their bare stomachs.

Upon seeing that the cannon had been re-directed, Graham stepped away from the mattress and concentrated his fire against Butch, who took cover behind a honeysuckle clump close by the cannon and began a rapid fire counter-attack. Lonnie continued to shoot at Carl, who waged an even more successful counterattack since Lonnie was the least experienced of all the warriors. The slingshots were deadly accurate, so all of the boys had to be nimble as they rose to shoot and then withdraw under cover to reload. The most dexterous of all the boys was Mister, who could frequently get off two shots before ducking behind the mulberry tree. He was also able to hold more berries in his cheeks than any other boy. None of the boys escaped getting hit, so all had a welt or two here and there.

At one point Graham got overconfident and moved far away from the mattress to get a better shot and caught one in the upper left arm, which caused him to jerk his arm downward. When he did he caught his wrist on the head of a nail on the front railing and cut it enough for blood to trickle down his arm. Since it didn't hurt much, Graham decided that the bloody wound added nicely to the atmosphere of the battle and continued firing.

Meanwhile Murray was ignoring any welts he received and concentrated on getting shots off at the chicken house. He got off two more before he realized that all he was doing was splattering mock orange juice all over the upslope of the tin roof. Todd and Ralph were able to toss a grenade between cannon shots, so Murray had to turn his back against the blast each time he reached for another mock orange. Thus, Murray was getting hit more than anyone else in the battle and soon yelled for Butch to run over to the chicken house to shoot the artillerymen. Running in a low crouch, Butch got over to the side of the building without getting hit, but as soon as he reached the down slope side of the chicken house he was hit by chinaberries from Todd and Ralph and had to run for cover in a nearby small grove of peach trees.

With a lull in the grenade attack, Murray ran around to the

front of the cannon and jerked out the rebar so he could re-position the cannon toward the tree house. Todd instructed Ralph to keep Butch occupied while Todd attempted the grenade attack alone. In the meantime Murray got hit a few times by Graham before he could get off another shot. Before he did, Graham yelled at Lonnie to get inside the mattress. Lonnie welcomed the chance to get under cover since he had been getting the worst of it from Carl. Taking a final shot at the receding figure of Lonnie, Carl ran back to the cannon to cover Murray.

When the mock orange took out the front railing and plowed into the mattress, both boys felt the mattress absorb the impact and heard the dull "whump!" While Murray was re-loading, both Graham and Lonnie stepped away from the mattress and fired two berries each, with Lonnie hitting Murray once, and Graham hitting Carl once and, off to his right, Sam once. Both Raiders got hit once each by Carl before ducking back inside the mattress to receive another mock orange blow. But this time Murray's aim was a little high, and the missile ricocheted off the top of the folded mattress and flew over the fence line into the hackberry trees on the west side property line. Graham felt the concussion and heard the missile whizzing by overhead and realized that the cannon had to be quieted soon, before someone got seriously hurt. As he ran to the front of the tree house before

Murray could re-load, he saw a grenade burst just above the cannon. He quickly got off a couple of shots at Sam while Lonnie focused his fire at Carl and Murray, who were busy ducking.

For the next several seconds Murray fumbled with replacing a rotten mock orange with a ripe one, while dodging or absorbing shots from Lonnie. His florid face was covered in sweat and sweat ran down his arms onto his palms. His movements became jerky as he shifted from wiping his hands on his pants and fumbling with the mock oranges and inner tube launcher. He was a study in frustration. Carl, his olive skin glistening with sweat, got little opposition from Lonnie, who found he preferred staying inside the mattress, even though the enclosed space under spotty shade was extremely hot. Only when the oppressive heat overcame his fear of Lonnie's chinaberries did he come out to take a shot. Consequently, Graham got more than half of Lonnie's shots

Mister and Blake poured as much firepower as they could at Sam. Graham alternated shooting at Carl and Sam, who was now caught in a crossfire. Tall and thin, his dirty blond hair plastered to his forehead by sweat, constantly ducking and weaving, Sam found little protection in the tall grass. Before Murray could get off another shot, Sam gave up his position and ran back to the cannon. Just as he arrived and turned around to look in the direction of Mister and Blake, he was hit in the back by a blast. The grenade exploded just three feet from him and tattooed mud and sand into his flesh. "Owww!!!" he screamed. Carl and Murray had heard the ominous whistle and ducked down and covered their heads. With Sam's withdrawal, Mister and Blake concentrated their fire at the cannon, as did Graham.

With Sam withdrawn to the cannon and Butch occupied over at the chicken house, all of the Raiders were emboldened to press their advantage. Mister and Blake looked like a pair of painted aborigines on their perch high in the mulberry tree. With the green mulberry branches sticking out of their sleeves, the purple mulberry juice on their flushed, sweaty faces now a scarlet color, they presented a formidable sight when they stepped away from the trunk of the tree and fired chinaberries down at the bunched Renegades.

Essentially unprotected under the onslaught of slingshot fire of four Raiders and the explosion of grenades, the Renegades were able to muster only a feeble defense, so Murray soon yelled "Retreat!"

The Retreat

RETREAT HAD NEVER BEEN CONSIDERED by the Renegades. There was no plan for orderly withdrawing and re-grouping. The four boys simply began running. Sam and Carl ran back the way they came, along the fence line. Murray ran through the neglected, overgrown Flournoy rose garden and through the side yard toward the highway. Butch left the peach tree grove and ran across the back yard to catch up with the fleeing older boy.

At that point Murray was convinced that the Raiders had fielded much older boys and he would be very sorry if he was captured and made a P.O.W. The year before when the Renegades had won they had captured one of the Raiders, tied him to a tree and tortured him by making him chew "elephant's ear," a highly astringent leaf that produced intense thirst. With their P.O.W begging for water, they

216

stood around him drinking from canteens, pouring water over their heads, and pouring it on the ground just inches from the suffering boy's mouth. Only after he yelled out that the Renegades were the best army in the world and the Raiders were a bunch of crybaby sissies did they give him any water and let him go.

As he ran along, Murray worried about retaliation that might be worse than what he had inflicted the year before. Butch could only think about sticking close to Murray.

When the Raiders saw the Renegades in full retreat they couldn't believe it at first, but then let out whoops of joy as they scampered down from their perches, stuffing chinaberries into their mouths as they ran after the retreating enemy. None of the six boys thought about going after Sam and Carl. They were enthralled with the idea of chasing Murray Austin and his sidekick, Butch.

Murray continued running across the highway and into Ruth's yard, with Butch close behind. As they ran alongside the windmill, both boys felt the sting of chinaberries hitting them and looked back to see all of the Raiders shooting at them while waiting on the other side of the road for a car to pass. Murray saw in a glance that there were no large boys among the pursuers and made an instant decision to stand and fight, so he veered off and ran behind Ruth's house, pulling out berries from one pocket and his slingshot from the other. He yelled at Butch to get ready to make a stand. Running wide open toward a large clump of pampas grass they could hide behind, he didn't see the water faucet sticking out of the ground, tripped on it and went sprawling onto the ground, slingshot and chinaberries scattered in front of him.

Butch caught up to him immediately and knelt down to see how badly he was hurt. Moaning loudly, Murray writhed in the dirt and spotty grass, blood oozing from the large cut on his ankle. In an instant they were surrounded by six Raiders, each aiming his stretched slingshot at the two on the ground. Since it was obvious that Murray and Butch were helpless, Graham shouted "At ease!" which was their signal to relax the tension in the slingshots.

With Murray moaning and Butch trying to comfort him, and Sam and Carl nowhere to be seen, Graham was trying to decide what to do next when the boys were surprised by the sudden appearance of Ruth St. John, who had quietly walked up and joined the circle.

THE TRUCE

"I WANT ALL OF YOU boys to go in that door there," indicating it with a nod of her head, "and wait for me in the kitchen while I get this young man off the ground and into the house." Looking directly at Butch, she said, "You stay and help me."

The boys did as they were told, opened the screen door, and filed into the kitchen, where they took seats on the floor at Graham's direction. All Ruth could hear as she and Butch helped Murray into the house was the squeaking of the screen door spring and the heavy breathing of the boys. Upon entering her kitchen, the only smell she was aware of was the pungent sweat of eight boys. She helped Murray to a seat at the table and invited Butch to join him.

"Would anybody like some iced tea?" Every hand except Murray's shot up. While she busied herself pouring the tea from the jug she kept in the refrigerator, she asked if there was anyone who could explain to her what was going on. After a few embarrassing moments, Graham spoke up,

"Miz St. John, we wuz just havin' our yearly slingshot battle with the Ramar Renegades. We have it every year. The Renegades wuz in retreat and we wuz chasin' 'em when Murray hurt his ankle."

He realized he still had his slingshot in his hand and quickly stuffed it in his pocket. Murray looked up and glared at him but dropped his head again and resumed moaning. After she had given out all the tea glasses, she opened the freezer compartment of her fridge and took out the ice trays so she could make a cold compress for Murray's ankle. She directed Butch to take the ice out of the trays and put them in the sink while she wet the corner of a dish towel. She told Murray to put his foot up on the table and began dabbing at the cut. When she was satisfied that the bleeding had stopped she placed the ice in the dish towel and placed the compress against Murray's ankle, which had already begun swelling and turning blue.

As her gaze shifted from one boy to the next, she said,

"My grandmother once told me about <u>her</u> grandmother seeing Indians dressed in war paint, but I don't think they could have looked more fearsome than you boys do." Shifting the compress around on the ankle, Ruth continued,

"Now tell me more about this annual war you boys have. I've been living in this house a long time, and I don't remember hearing about any war."

"It's not a war, Miz St. John, it's a chinaberry battle. It's just a rivalry between them and us. We don't mean to do anybody any harm," said Graham.

"Don't you know you could put out an eye with those... slingshots?" Three of the boys sitting on the floor slid their slingshots behind their backs.

"That sounds pretty harmful to me. But my guess is that you've been told this by your mamas already. Tell me more about this battle." First Graham, then Todd, then Butch tried to explain what the battle was all about, but they tended just to repeat what the previous boy had said.

Ruth decided you just had to be a boy to understand, so she told them the battle that year was over and for them to go home and get cleaned up. She wanted them back at her house the next day so she could teach them how to play croquet, hoping as she spoke that she could find the set she had bought twenty years before when Cousin Bea's children were small. She then said if they were not there by ten a.m. she would call their parents to ask if they are sick. Then she excused them, and the boys filed slowly out of her kitchen with their heads down, feeling neither victorious nor defeated. Only Graham and Todd had ever played croquet,

221

so for most of them it would be a new experience--but not one they looked forward to. The dominant thought among the boys was that this is no way to end a chinaberry battle!

Two Misfits Become Friends

When Murray took down his foot and tried to stand, Ruth told him to stay awhile, so he sat back down and put his foot back on the table, folded his arms, and stared at the floor. After all the other boys left, she asked him if he had any pain. When he said yes, she went to her medicine chest and brought back two aspirin, which she gave him with a glass of iced tea.

"What is your name, child?"

"Murray, ma'am,"

"Last name?"

"Austin"

"You look too old to be playing with those other boys. How old are you?"

"Fourteen, ma'am."

"Those other boys don't look to be more than ten. Why do you play with boys so much younger than you?"

After taking a long drink from his ice tea glass to buy time, "I dunno. I just like the younger boys."

Ruth fingered her pearl necklace and stared intently at Murray, as her interest in him keened, while he kept his head down. A thought quickly crossed her mind that she would have made a great mother. "You must have friends your own age at school."

"Yes, ma'am, but they aren't really friends. They're just in my classes."

"Why aren't they your friends?"

Murray began squirming in his chair, wishing she would tell him to go home, too. "They make fun of my clothes. They tease me about the food I bring from home. Sometimes I have to miss school when they don't get to miss, and they pick on me when I get back."

Ruth reflected on this for a while, then said, "Are you Jewish, Murray?"

"Yes, ma'am"

"What about the synagogue? Aren't there any Jewish children your age there?"

"No'm. Just a girl. She's fifteen. And a few babies."

Ruth found herself growing increasingly more sympathetic with Murray. She thought back to when she was fourteen and how much she felt like a misfit, too. Whereas she didn't think Murray had fully entered puberty yet, with all the complications that brings, her hormones raged at that age. But she was kept under very strict control by her mother, her grandmother--and her own conscience. In the year following her first kiss with Ray Lee, she had grown two inches and was a head taller than all the boys in her class and most of the girls. She felt awkward and gangly and often overreacted to imagined offenses.

One day when she was in a stall in the girl's restroom between classes she overheard Missy Demeret talking to two of the girls in her clique as they entered the bathroom,

"That Ruth St. John is such a bother," using a term she had recently heard in a British movie. "She's beginning to look like a cow with those abnormal breasts of hers. And the way she slouches when she walks makes me wonder if she doesn't need milking!"

All three girls started laughing at the image of Ruth being milked. Ruth sat quietly in the stall, embarrassed to be seen coming out of it, but being the butt of ridicule made her angry. She felt her face redden, and she began gritting her teeth. All three girls were primping in front of the mirrors when Ruth stormed out of the stall and stalked over to Missy. She grabbed the collar of Missy's blue and white sailor's jumper and spun her around. She pressed her nose against Missy's and said,

"If I'm a cow, Missy Demeret, then you are a snake! You are long and slender with no figure at all! Somebody needs to step on you!" Then she stalked out of the restroom. She was so angry that she forgot to regain her composure once outside, and the other students in the hallway gave her a wide berth. Before the day was finished the whole school was talking about the "fight" between Ruth and Missy.

By the time she reached high school, and the other girls had caught up to her, and the boys had grown taller than she was, the damage had been done. With many of the students she carried the image of an awkward, overdeveloped, easily angered girl. A few began referring to her as Ruthless Ruth.

Ruth fingered her pearl necklace and just stared at the condensation on the side of her glass while re-living that scene with Missy so long ago. Murray was relieved just to be able to quietly stare at the flower patterns on the linoleum-covered floor. Rachael, two years younger, was slow entering puberty. During the time Ruth felt like an oversexed freak, Rachael was still petite and pretty. Her transition to womanhood proved to be much smoother than Ruth's.

When her thoughts came back to the present, Ruth pondered what to say to this plump, pathetic child. She was suddenly reminded of something she had recently seen in the newspaper. The Boy Scouts would be marching in the annual Fourth of July parade down Marshall Boulevard. Maybe she could interest him in joining the Boy Scouts.

"Murray, are you in the Boy Scouts?"

"No'm"

"Have you ever thought about joining the Scouts?"

"No'm"

"I think you would enjoy Scouting very much. They go camping in the forest. They earn merit badges for learning about plants and animals. They have what they call jamborees, when thousands of them get together and hear speeches from famous men who have been Scouts themselves. Some of those men are Jews."

Murray's interest perked up a bit, and he raised his head and looked at her. "I know about the Boy Scouts, but I never thought they would let me in because I'm a Jew. I've always liked bein' out-uh-doors...Once when we wuz down at Grandaddy's farm, Daddy got me up real early in the mornin' when you could just barely see, and we went for a long walk across the pasture into the woods. We stopped in a little clearin' and Daddy cleared away the leaves to make a spot for a campfire. Then he took some stones from a creek over a ways and put them in a small circle inside the big circle. That's where he built a fire out of dried leaves and dead limbs. When the fire was goin' good, he pulled a big, black fryin' pan out of his croaker sack and put it on top of the stones..." Looking wistfully back at the floor, Murray concluded, "And the whole time he was doin' that, he wuz tellin' me about nature and Indians and livin' off the land. He fixed us some hash and potatoes, scrambled eggs, toast, orange juice...That was the best breakfast I ever had."

"What is your father's name, and your mother's?"

"Frank and Sara. Austin"

"I'm going to call your parents and talk to them about getting you in the Scouts. Then I'm going to call up the man who heads the local troop. By the way, where do you live?"

"I live over in Ramar."

"That's a long way from here. You traveled all the way over here to do battle with these local boys?

"Yes, ma'am." He didn't dare tell her that he brought his own army and a mock orange cannon. At the thought of the cannon left in the Flournoy back field, he let out a low moan.

"Is your ankle hurting more?"

"Yes, ma'am."

"I can't give you any more aspirin, so I better send you home. It's much too far for you to walk with a hurt ankle, so I'm gonna call my Cousin Bea and get her to drive you home."

"Yes, ma'am," he said, while quickly considering what kind of reaction he could expect from his mother.

Soon after Cousin Bea drove away with Murray lying in the back seat, Ruth decided she better call the local office of the Scouts before calling Mr. and Mrs. Austin. She wanted to make sure they would accept Jewish boys.

(Ring)

"Mayor's office"

"Yes, this is Ruth St. John. Is the mayor in?"

Recognizing one of the city's most prominent citizens, the secretary felt it was worth interrupting the mayor's meeting with the chief of police, so she pressed the intercom button and told him who was calling on line #2.

"Hello, Ruth. Howya been?"

"I'm just fine, Howard, despite having a few teeth loosened by being bounced through the potholes in the city's streets in my cousin's car."

"Oh, c'mon, Ruth. We got some of the best paved streets in the state. What can I do for you?"

"I've just acquired a young Jewish friend, and I want to know if he can get into any of the Boy Scout Troops in Riverton."

"A young Jewish friend? How young?"

"Fourteen."

"Jewish?"

"Yes"

"Well, that's a question I've not received before. But I don't see any problem with it. It's not like the Scouts are goin' to be taken over by Jews."

"Can I count on him being admitted to the closest one to Ramar, where he lives?"

..."Yes, you can."

"Thank you. My best to Eileen"

"You're quite welcome. Anytime"

Forty minutes later she got a call from Stan Lipkowitz, Scout Master for the Ramar District, sponsored by the Kiwanis Club. After a brief conversation in which Ruth gave him the particulars, it was decided that Murray could be admitted and that Ruth would call his parents to discuss his joining.

Ruth had a pleasant conversation with Sara Austin, who agreed to let Murray join the Scouts. Ruth then gave her the number for Mr. Lipkowitz.

After her phone call she looked around for the croquet set then remembered she had stored it in the attic, so she called the Flournoy house and had Graham come over to climb up into the attic and retrieve the set. While up there Graham was tempted to stay a while and look at all the interesting things he saw. There were two steamer trunks against a wall, both covered with dust and spider webs. The possible contents of those trunks intrigued him. In a dark corner Graham was startled by a ghost-like wire mannequin supporting a wedding dress yellow with age. His fascination with the strange objects he saw distracted him from the intense heat and dust, but he tarried so long that Ruth called up to ask if he was okay. He grabbed the croquet set just inside the opening and climbed back down to the cool of the hallway.

While he was in the attic Ruth had decided that as long as she had this strong, healthy boy she would get him to set up the croquet in her back yard. For the next half-hour Ruth directed while Graham did the bending to get the hoops inserted in the spotty grass in her yard. The next morning at the appointed time, except for Murray, all of the Renegades and Raiders showed up.

After a few minutes of instruction from Ruth, they started. Though there were no teams, the Renegades and Raiders were nevertheless in competition with each other and would be easy on each other and hard on the "enemy." At one point Ruth had to scold Sam for trying to knock Blake's ball into the highway. While this was going on Butch sidled up to Todd and muttered, "Wait'll next year!" and Todd responded in a loud whisper, "Better bring a bigger cannon!"

JANE'S CANADIAN SUMMER

UNLIKE THE CHILDREN, WHO BARELY noticed the weather, the adults in Riverton wilted in the relentless, humid heat. Many cursed when the radio weatherman announced the "start" of summer on June 21st. They would have resented Jane Forrester, now living in cool, dry bliss. The average summer day in Lawrence Refuge hovered around seventy degrees, with low humidity.

Dressed in stockings and low heel shoes, a gray wool skirt, a blue, long-sleeved blouse and a white cardigan sweater, Jane was perched on a rocky promontory overlooking the sea. She relished the cool breezes that brushed her cheeks and caressed her hair. During her ten days there she had moved from the hotel to a small boarding house in town operated by a middle-aged widow. The only other tenant, Alice, had just completed her first year teaching at the elementary school.

Ben, about sixty, did handyman jobs for the widow between trips on his fishing boat. His manner was as gentle as his hands were rough. The young lover she told Bob about in the letter was forged in her heated, vindictive imagination.

Over those cool, carefree days her thoughts had mellowed, and as she sat looking out at the dark, brooding sea and gentle, foamy surf, she decided that she had been immature and self-centered. Yes, she did have a legitimate grievance against the people who had controlled her life. But maybe she had been unfair. She may have exaggerated the danger Bob posed to her. She still felt guilty about her mother and brother.

Alice, out for a walk on the beach road, saw Jane sitting on the rock.

"Jane?"

"Oh!...hello, Alice." For a split second, lost in thought back in Riverton, Jane thought that her mother had called out her name.

"Do you mind if I sit for a while?"

"Of course not," said Jane as she scooted over on the blanket to make room for the younger woman, patting the spot next to her.

As she took her seat on the blanket, Alice continued, "I know you must be feeling a lot of pain now that you've lost your husband."

This was the first time anyone had inquired about her feelings as a new "widow," and Jane hadn't prepared any response. The occasional "I'm sorry for your grief" or "God bless you" called for little more than a "Thank you."

"Well...yes, it does hurt, Alice...But being in this beautiful country has lessened the pain considerably (too bland, she thought). I miss him a great deal, but when the hurt gets bad, I just think about all the good years we had together and be thankful for them. What about you? Where is your home?"

"I'm from a village close to London, Ontario, just north of Detroit. I've always wanted to be a teacher and to travel. I love my teaching job here in Lawrence Refuge, but one day I would like to go to someplace exotic to teach."

"I envy you, Alice," Jane said, as she looked wistfully out to sea. "My life was pretty much planned for me. You have choices. I had none."

"You have choices now," said Alice, while testing the softness of the blanket with her hand. "You chose to leave the South and move to Canada."

"Right now I'm here as a visitor. If I want to stay permanently I'll have to apply for Canadian citizenship. I love this Canadian summer, but I may want to go back home to Alabama once I see a Canadian winter."

"They're not so bad if you know how to dress properly.

It's also important not to do certain things. I hope you don't lick flagpoles in the winter."

Jane turned her face toward Alice and smiled, "No, I gave up that hobby a couple of years ago."

"How cold does it get in Alabama?"

"It rarely gets below freezing in Riverton. We have many winter days when you can play tennis."

"What about swimming?"

"No, if you want to swim you have to go to south Florida, a coupla hundred miles to the south. What about your love life, Alice? Any young men in your life?"

Alice blushed and turned her face away. "No, nobody serious." Turning back to face Jane, "I don't want to get serious with anyone. I want to travel."

As they continued to talk, Jane could sense a bit of conflict in Alice's remarks. She wants to have an exciting life, experience new things, but she also wants the security and predictability of family life with a husband and children. This was a conflict Jane had never experienced.

In a lull in the conversation both women stared at the horizon, at the sharp line between the dark blue water and the light blue sky, as though waiting for Neptune to tell them what to do with their lives.

They spent a pleasant two hours talking and watching the sun sink closer to the Bay of Fundy, and Jane couldn't remember the last time she enjoyed herself so much. The air was fresh, and the smell of the sea was pleasant and evocative of strange lands. Alice giggled when asking for translations of Jane's southern pronunciations and expressions like "fixin' to." Jane teased Alice when "about" came out "aboot" and other Canadian pronunciations. She learned that Alice was young enough to be her daughter and, during the course of their conservation, Jane began to feel a mother's fondness for this petite, personable young woman so far from home. Without realizing what she was doing, Jane raised her right arm and put it around Alice's shoulders. As she did so the white cardigan sweater fell from her shoulders onto the blanket and Alice leaned, almost imperceptibly, toward Jane.

SAYING NO TO JIM CROW

BACK IN RIVERTON, GAYLE FREEMONT was preparing an article for <u>Geosciences Today</u>. Because his teaching, advising, and committee work took so much time during the school year, Gayle saved his "publish or perish" work for the summer. He lived in an apartment above the garage behind the house of his landlord, Professor Martinez, the head of foreign languages at St. Luke. Gayle was also writing letters of application to several colleges and universities in the north and west. His resolve to escape the Jim Crow South was undiminished, despite the temptation to get "entangled" with Angelina Roberts, the daughter of one of his colleagues at the college.

Taking a break from his writing, and needing some cooler air, he walked out of the apartment onto the landing at the head of the wooden stairway on the outside of the garage.

He stretched and yawned then leaned against the railing. He peered at the evening sky just over the huge crape myrtle tree next to the stairway. The scentless pink flowers took on a salmon color in the fading light. From off in a neighboring yard came the musty sweet scent of magnolia flowers. Gayle had seen the tree in the backyard of a spooky, two-story white frame house down the street, with upper and lower verandahs across the front. The tree was taller than the house and almost as wide. It reminded him of a magnolia he played in as a child in New Orleans.

The sky was partially blocked by a thirty-foot pecan tree at the bottom of the yard to his left, but there was enough open space to his right to see a large patch of sky. As he stared at the sky, hundreds of stars began to appear as the last traces of sunlight disappeared. In this residential neighborhood there was very little artificial light to detract from the luster of the stars. They got no competition from the moon, which was low on the horizon behind the trees.

The idea that each little star had to compete with other light sources in order to shine reminded him of his effort to make his own little star shine. He drew in a deep breath and reflected on his life circumstances.

He had met Angelina at a recent faculty party at the home of her parents and fell under her spell. She had recently graduated from Spelman College in Atlanta and was currently doing volunteer work and helping her father with some of his administrative duties at the college. Her most attractive feature was her smile. It was broad, and her teeth were even and gloriously white against her bronze skin. Her laugh was spontaneous and rich. Many young women he had known "faked" their smiles and laughs in a noticeably affected manner. But hers were utterly natural. He sensed no affectation at all, and this alone charmed him. They had dated a few times, and he had kissed her goodnight on their last date. Her kiss, like her laugh and smile, was natural, genuinely responsive and affectionate. There was nothing devious about this girl.

Unfortunately, after the kiss they had talked briefly about the future and he discovered that Angelina was committed to staying in the South, close to her family and friends. She had laughed that wonderful laugh when he casually queried her about living in another section of the country. The spontaneity of her laugh convinced him that it had probably never occurred to her to live anywhere else.

Thus, Gayle Freemont stood at a fork in the road. Go right and he would avoid entanglements like Angelina and take a faculty position at a college up north or out west. He could make annual visits to New Orleans to see his family. He would be free of the constraints put on "colored" men in the South.

People like Angelina, her parents and many other black people he knew were content to live in a parallel universe where they could move freely up the social and career ladders, apart from the white world. Yes, it was more difficult seeing "Whites Only" at every turn, but the black people had created an elaborate network that allowed them to move rather freely despite the legal segregation. They just had to know the places where they were welcome, who the contacts were, and how to act when dealing with white people. Preserving one's dignity under such a complicated and artificial system had become an art form.

Go left and he would remain just another "nigger" or the more respectful "nigra" or "colored man." The white community would not recognize him as Dr. Freemont or even Mr. Freemont. He would be just Gayle. Yes, he could hide out in the parallel universe of Colored Society and avoid white people, but he was convinced that racial segregation should end, and it was up to young, progressive blacks like himself to make it happen. But he would not do his fighting in hostile territory. He would "go west, young man"-—or north.

Taking one last deep breath of the sweet night air and stretching out his arms to refresh his muscles, he walked back into the apartment to continue his letter: "My personal interests include reading, hiking, tennis..."

A Trip to the Beach to Get a Tan...and a Man?

With the end-of-year school paperwork done, as well as neglected chores around her duplex, Priscilla Andrews invited her fellow teacher, Anne Bonair, to join her in a trip to Panama City, Florida, not far to the south of Riverton. They loaded up Anne's '37 Plymouth with suitcases, blankets, suntan lotion, a beach umbrella, beach towels, food, beer, and a tabletop radio.

It being late June, they hoped their pupils had already been to the beach and wouldn't see their teachers in swimsuits. They would be wearing sunglasses not only to block the intense sunlight, and to look a bit mysterious, but also to disguise themselves. The trip was uneventful except for nearly hitting a white sharecropper's hound on one of the back roads they took to get to the main highway.

Alice swerved sharply to avoid the dog when he appeared suddenly out of the tall Johnson grass on the side of the road. They slowed down and looked back to see if the dog had been hurt at all, and both the dog and its apparent owner seemed not to have noticed the near miss. They just stood in a cloud of dust looking up the road at their car.

Less than three hours later they pulled into Panama City and stopped for gas. As they pulled away from the station, Anne exclaimed, "Thirty-five cents a gallon for regular gas! I sure couldn't afford to live down here!" She wanted to say something to the attendant while he was checking her tires and oil and radiator water. But he was a well mannered, pleasant, middle-aged man, and she decided that the outrageous pricing was not his fault. She felt a little better as they got closer to Panama City Beach and she could smell the salt air.

They found the weathered, gray, beach cottage rustic but serviceable. Upon entering they immediately noticed the strong odor of mildew. The cottage had one bedroom and two fold-up beds against the wall in the pine-paneled living room. The small kitchen was separated from the living room by a kitchen bar with stools, where one could sit and eat or read. Under one of the windows at the east end of the living room was a kitchen table covered by a red oilcloth adorned with yellow daisies, and four chairs. A couch, a bookcase and a suitcase table occupied other spaces on the wall of the living room. The front and back of the cottage had both solid doors and screen doors. They could open both ends of the cottage to get cross ventilation without admitting insects. A ceiling fan would also help dispel the relentless heat of the beach.

Anne placed the radio on the table and plugged it into the wall socket under the oilcloth. After tuning in a local station, she busied herself putting kitchen goods on the shelves and in the small refrigerator. When a vocal group began singing,"Please, Mr. May-truh-dee, a cold collard sandwich for my baby and me," she joined in while doing a little dance, "for dee-zert, by and by, a nice, fat piece of persimmon pie!" From the bedroom where she was putting away their clothes, Priscilla called out, "You're making me hungry!" So they hurriedly finished putting away their clothes, beach supplies, and toiletries so they could get to supper.

At first they thought they should try to fix something there rather than go out but soon convinced themselves that they didn't have to get that dressed up. After all, they were at the beach where casual was the watchword. They had seen Molly's Seafood Palace coming in and their mouths watered for "Florida lobster" (crayfish tails), fried oysters, fried shrimp, hush puppies, and all the rest. There was also the possibility they might meet a man at Molly's. As she pulled out of their parking space and drove toward the beach highway, Anne tried to put a tune to "Meeting a Man at Molly's."

The next morning they gathered up all their beach material and walked through the hot, heavy, white sand, to the top of a sand dune, through a patch of sea oats, to a flat area just above the reach of the surf. "Let me rub some of this lotion on your back, Anne," said Priscilla. When it was Priscilla's turn to get slathered, Anne chattered happily, not being especially careful to avoid getting lotion on the swimsuit. Adjusting her sunglasses with the back of her hand, she said,

"Prissy, why don't you just remove the top of your suit so I don't get any lotion on it. You could get an even tan and be a local sensation at the same time!"

"That's a great idea, Anne! Maybe we should just go all the way and lay out here in the nude. But later we would have a hard time getting a tan while sitting in a jail cell. And speaking of indecent exposure, we better be careful not to get burned. If we do, we're gonna look like lepers rather than movie stars when we get back."

Priscilla's interest in getting a decent tan was more than a movie star look. She had learned that a proper tan helped erase the ugliness of her acne scars. Through tanning, all of the skin on her face took on a uniform reddish-tan color, which made her more attractive. Her chestnut brown hair was nice and thick and shoulder length, and her figure, on her 5'10" frame, was large but attractive. Because of her height she was often tempted to slump, but she was intelligent enough to know that such behavior was not only excessively vain but could also be injurious to her spine. So she forced herself to stand erect. Standing tall also made her an imposing figure to her pupils, which lent to the respect she enjoyed, and it was a good example to them to maintain proper posture.

At only 5'4" with blonde hair, blue eyes, and fair skin, Anne fit the ideal much better than she did, but Anne's fair skin made her more susceptible to sunburn. After they finished rubbing lotion on each other's back, Anne leaned back on extended arms and said, "Well, we're here. Where are the men?"

"They're with their wives or off fishing or still at work. Not much chance of meeting available men at the end of June in the middle of the week," Priscilla groused.

Almost as if on cue, a surprisingly attractive man about their age strolled into view looking intently at the wet sand left behind as the surf slid out to sea. Occasionally he would stoop quickly and probe the sand with a trowel. In his other hand was a rusty child's sand bucket.

"Do you see a wedding band?" said Anne.

"I haven't noticed his <u>hands</u> yet," Priscilla said with a snicker. Why don't you go out into the surf and yell for help. While he's carrying you in you can have a good look at his hands."

Covered only by form-fitting white swim trunks, his tanned and trim, sweat-suffused, muscular body glistened in the sunlight, and his right tricep muscle bunched sexily with each thrust of the trowel into the wet sand. His abundant light brown hair waved seductively in the gentle ocean breeze. The women found themselves sitting up a little straighter, preening, hoping he would at least glance their way.

On the verge of initiating a conversation with him as he moved farther down the beach, they were surprised at the sudden appearance of another, equally attractive man, who engaged the first man in conversation they couldn't hear. Then the two men began strolling away from them, side by side. As they did, the first man stole a glance back at Priscilla and Anne and smiled. Then, to their shock and amazement, he ran his index finger down the other man's spine and gave him a quick pat on the rump.

The women had little knowledge of and no previous experience with homosexuality and weren't exactly sure of what they were seeing. They just sat there stunned for several seconds before Anne said, "Prissy, did you see what I saw? Did we just see a couple of queers?"

"I think we did," was Priscilla's expressionless reply. "I

didn't know they could be so good looking. I thought they were all puny, mousy little men. How in the world are we supposed to find a man when we have to compete not only with other women but other good looking men?"

UFOs at Tax Time

RAYMOND LEWIS HAD ENJOYED HAVING Jesse help with the business paperwork. Ray didn't have much patience with legalese and tax instructions, so getting Jesse's help had given him more time to do what he loved best, getting his hands in the dirt. With both a flower shop and a greenhouse to operate, Raymond had little time to work with his plants, so finding out about Jesse's skills was a pleasant discovery. He was forced to see Jesse in a whole different light. He was forced to give him his own classification, unique in Raymond's experience: a "nigra" who was just like a white man.

His experience with blacks his whole life had convinced him that they would avoid work whenever possible, and when you could get them to work they couldn't be trusted to do a job right without supervision. But Jesse had always not only done the work required of him but could do it without supervision. He would also do work not asked of him but needed to be done. For a couple of years Raymond had been thinking about putting Jesse in charge of the greenhouse, supervising three other blacks, and he would supervise the flower shop. But he didn't think Jesse was smart enough. Now that he had been elevated to "Greenhouse Worker and Reader," Raymond felt a lot better about promoting him, and would speak to him soon about it.

Jesse not only liked the extra money he was making, he was also proud that a white man respected him enough to trust him with important business matters. He too had thought about being made supervisor of the greenhouse but never thought Raymond would promote a black man. Now that he was being trusted with business paperwork he felt better about maybe suggesting the arrangement to his boss. One day at quitting time, Jesse reminded Ray that quarterly tax reports were due on the first of July.

"Hmmm, yeah, I guess I been puttin' you off about that, Jes. Whaddaya say we work on them tonight? I'll put you on the clock when we start."

"That'll be fine, Mr. Ray. I'll shuffle over here after supper. What time will you be here?"

"What about six-thirty?"

"Fine with me."

It was six twenty-five p.m., June 25, 1947, and the moist heat was palpable when Ray pulled up to the greenhouse in his Chevy. He just sat there for several seconds wondering how it could be so warm so late in the day. Jesse was already seated at the little desk in the corner they used as an office when Ray walked up.

"These accounts receivable numbers look about right, Mr. Ray." For the next two hours the two men sat at the desk, side by side, knee to knee, and fumbled with receipts and invoices as they steadily worked their way through the officious maze of tax instructions.

Just after full dark, both men were surprised by a bright light shining down through the greenhouse glass. At first Jesse thought it was somebody hunting illegally with a spotlight, but how could that be when the light was directly above them? The hunters couldn't be up in a tree. Ray thought at first that a full moon had suddenly broken free of clouds but soon realized it was more like sunlight than moonlight. Stunned and perplexed, both men just sat there looking up through the glass, their mouths hanging open.

Then, simultaneously, they jumped out of their metal folding chairs and ran outside to see what it could be. There, off to the west, maybe fifty feet off the ground, was a cigar-shaped object hovering silently above a row of loblolly pines. There were five, large, very bright white lights along the bottom of the object and three red lights, two at the front of the row and one at the back. Considering the spaces between the pines they knew so well, they each calculated to themselves that the object was about sixty feet long and fifteen to twenty feet wide. It made absolutely no sound. The two men were aware only of their labored breathing and the drone of the insects and tree frogs. The night creatures didn't seem to notice the intruder. After what seemed to be hours the right end of the object turned toward them, and they saw its cylindrical shape. It appeared to be about fifteen feet in diameter. Shortly after turning toward them it rose slowly and silently for several feet then sped away. In less than one second it was out of sight.

Neither Ray nor Jesse had heard of the "flying saucer" sighting the day before by a pilot, Kenneth Arnold, flying near Mt. Rainier, Washington, so they had no preparation for what they had just witnessed. They just stood there and stared at the spot above the pines where the object had been. After a minute of silent searching, Ray mumbled something to Jesse and, zombie-like, made his way to his car, got in and drove away at ten miles an hour. Jesse just stood there and watched Ray until his car disappeared, then, also zombie-like, he walked home along the dusty dirt road, head down, deep in thought.

The next day both arrived at the greenhouse earlier than

usual, sat down and finished preparing the taxes. Neither one mentioned the incident, each preferring to dismiss it as a dream, both afraid to acknowledge what they knew was impossible. Each man also feared that the other man hadn't seen it. But it didn't take long before each man saw the haunted look in the other man's eyes and knew they had a shared experience that would link them for the rest of their lives.

On the edges of his mind Ray realized that if what he saw was real, he had witnessed the existence of a vastly superior race. In the face of that, the differences between him and Jesse, if any, disappeared. Jesse's thoughts were similar. It occurred to him that if what they had seen was from a superior civilization, then the exalted status of white people was undeserved.

MURRAY AND RUTH

AFTER TAKING CARE OF MURRAY on the day of the chinaberry battle, and arranging for him to join the Boy Scouts, Ruth couldn't get the boy out of her mind. In some ways he reminded her of Ray Lee Johnson, the boy who had kissed her in the privet hedge so many years ago. Murray sort of looked like Ray, with his reddish hair, and their mannerisms were similar. Ruth decided that Murray could be his grandson if Ray Lee hadn't died in the Spanish American War. Maybe because of Ray Lee, maybe because she saw her younger self in Murray, she decided to continue helping him.

Ruth dialed the Austins' telephone number. Sara answered the phone.

"Mrs. Austin?

"Yes"

"This is Ruth St. John . I called you several days ago about Murray joining the Boy Scouts. Did he get in okay?"

"Yes, Miz St. John, and I thank you again for taking such an interest in the boy. I'm sorry Murray caused you so much trouble, and I'm much obliged for the care you gave his injured foot."

"It was no trouble, and I enjoyed getting to know the young man. I'm a maiden lady with no children in my life, and talking to your son reminded me of what I have been missing. I wonder if you would mind if I do some things for him."

"No...No, that would be fine. What do you have in mind?"

"Well, I have an A.B. degree from Flo Hennessy College if he ever needs any help with his homework. Can't say I'd be much help with his math, but I might be able to help him with his English or history."

"That's mighty kind of you, Miss St. John. I'll let Murray know of your offer. I'm happy to say that he does rather well in school, but there just might be something you could do. His daddy and me don't have much education, so we can't help him much. Thank you kindly."

Thus began a relationship that soon made Ruth a kind of grandmother to him. Murray's maternal grandparents in Detroit had never accepted their daughter's gentile Southern family. As for his paternal grandparents, who lived ten miles away on a farm out in the country, Murray was the child of a "Yankee Jewess." They had never rejected Murray and his mother, but they had never warmly accepted them either.

Murray Austin's father Frank grew up on that farm. He could remember when River Road had only a few country estates close to the Aldrich Plantation. It was the only paved road for miles around, because it was also US 177 to Florida. He recalled how nice it was when he was a boy to finally get off the rut-filled dirt roads onto the smooth ribbon of asphalt. Riding along comfortably with his dad in their Model T Ford, he marveled at the country estates and longed to live in one himself.

By the time he was twenty-one the Great Depression had crushed the economy of Blalock County. After trying for several months to get any kind of work locally, he jumped a train going north and made his way to Detroit. There he was offended by "uppity niggers," but he was able to get work as a garbage man in one of the better neighborhoods. It galled him to have to work for a black driver, but it was a job. In Riverton all garbage trucks were driven by white men, and black men collected the garbage.

He lived in a rooming house where he also got an evening meal. On his way to work he would stop by Bertalloni's Deli and pick up a corned beef sandwich for his lunch and maybe a sweet roll for his breakfast. It was there that he met Sara Zuckermann, who worked behind the counter. After knowing each other for only a couple of months they decided to get married over the stern objections of Sara's Jewish family. Frank's family was not informed of the decision in the occasional postcard Frank sent home. When Sara got pregnant, and the Zuckermanns threatened to disown her, Frank decided to take his wife home to Blalock County.

After a year of living with Frank's parents and Frank going from one sales job to another, Blalock Mills posted a few job openings. Frank applied in sanitation, having acquired experience in the garbage business. Through hard work and a willingness to learn, Frank not only held on to his job but managed to rise up in the company over the next dozen years. His biggest advancement was to line assistant in 1942 when the mill got a huge government contract for military apparel. Now in his thirteenth year with the company he was finally comfortable. Although they had no more children, Sara was content being a mill wife and mother of Murray, and doing volunteer work at Temple B'nai Israel, the only synagogue in Riverton.

Having no other Jewish children in his neighborhood or his school, Murray did not connect to his Jewish heritage, despite his mother's efforts. He wished he were not a Jew. He would even sometimes go to church services with his Christian friends to draw attention from his Jewish identity.

With Sara Austin's support and encouragement, Ruth began a personal project to do for Murray what no one had ever done for her: help him deal with a world that could often be cruel. She encouraged him to be proud of his religion, and with Cousin Bea as chauffer she took him to the Carnegie Library and showed him books that chronicled the history of the Jewish people. She showed him magazine articles about the emerging state of Israel and such heroes as David Ben Gurion. She avoided sources dealing with the Holocaust, preferring to emphasize the positive aspects of his heritage. He would learn about all that soon enough she decided. She had him check out a couple of books on the history of his people and their contribution to the development of the United States of America.

She took him shopping for clothes that would look good on him. She knew it was only a matter of time before he would take a serious interest in girls, and she wanted him to be better prepared than she was when the time came. She wanted him to date and one day marry a nice woman (not necessarily Jewish) and have a nice family life. She told him that he would look better if he could lose a little weight, and they would go shopping again when he needed smaller sizes.

"Murray, what is this fascination with slingshot battles?"

Ruth asked him one day while on a picnic in the city park. Ruth and Bea had prepared a picnic lunch at Ruth's house and were spreading it out on the slightly warped wood table in the shade of several large blackjack oak trees. She asked the question as she set down the plate of pineapple sandwiches (Murray's favorite). Murray was seated at the bench already and reached for a sandwich before answering. Ruth popped his hand and told him to wait until after the blessing. While removing the ice tea jug from the basket, Bea stole a glance at the pair and smiled with satisfaction that Ruth had become so like a grandmother.

"I dunno, Miz Ruth. The excitement I guess. I love the challenge of beatin' the Raiders, and I look forward to the battle all year. This was my fourth year fightin' and my second year as commander. I like bein' in charge. I like gettin' respect."

"Don't you think it's time you gave up the fightin'? You'll be fifteen years old soon," Ruth said soothingly as she poured tea into his glass.

"I could think better on a full stomach," said Murray.

"Okay. Bea, would you say the blessing?" Ruth said as she awkwardly maneuvered herself onto the bench that was mounted to the side of the table.

After they finished eating and had put the picnic goods back in the car, the three of them strolled through the zoo section of the park. A nearby dome-shaped cage was twenty feet high and forty feet in diameter. Constructed of thick iron bars that converged at the top, the cage covered a dirt floor and scattered shrubs and pine seedlings. A four-foot fence prevented the spectators from getting too close. Between the fence and the cage was a grassy ten-foot section of "no man's land." It occurred to Bea that a cage that imposing must house King Kong. She was a little disappointed when they saw two adult black bears appear from behind what appeared to be some kind of concrete cave. They strolled along the path, in single file, and grunted with each step.

The monkey cages were more interesting, as there was a great deal of activity and chatter. The cages were less imposing than the bear cage but had the same barrier between the cage and the spectators. Ruth wondered which species was being protected by the safety zone, the humans or the monkeys.

When Bea saw a spider monkey masturbating, she quickly directed the attention of Murray and Ruth to a trio of capuchins grooming each other. Ruth bought a bag of roasted peanuts from a nearby vendor and gave it to Murray, who enjoyed eating one and then trying to throw one between the bars to the monkeys. Some of the capuchins stuck their little hands through the bars and tried to catch the nut before it could reach the others. Any monkey that got a peanut raced up and down the "monkey bars" shrieking in delight at both getting the treat and keeping it away from the others. Murray couldn't help but notice the similarity between the monkeys and many human children, himself included.

On the other side of the monkey cages was a fenced concrete pool for alligators. It was twenty feet in diameter and four feet deep. Between the pool and stout metal bars was a grassy area where the alligators could sun themselves. One of those sunbathing looked to be twenty feet long.

"Don't throw peanuts at the alligators, Murray. They don't like peanuts but some birds do. How would you like for one of these pigeons to fly in there to get a meal and become a meal itself?"

"Sorry, Miz Ruth, but as big as that one is I think a pigeon would just be a snack. He would need uh ostrich."

"Smart Alec!" said Ruth, smiling.

Ruth and Bea enjoyed the stroll through the botanical gardens, a welcome reprieve from the strong animal odors. Some of the plants, such as the Confederate Jasmine, gave off a pleasant scent. In late winter the gardens had been a jungle of camellias and azaleas. Now it was filled with roses of every hue, and gardenia and crape myrtle and dwarf magnolia. The women paused at each variety to sample their beauty and scent. Murray rapidly lost interest and picked up several pieces of gravel from the path and began throwing the rocks at large trees and trash cans. Ruth soon put a stop to that, and he began dragging his feet.

Soon they came to the stone pavilion where exotic plants were on display. Park officials were lecturing on the plants, and Murray's interest in plants perked up when they got to the Venus Flytrap demonstration. Murray even got to feed it a dead fly.

After their very busy day at the park they strolled back to the parking lot. It was time to take Murray home. All of them were tired, and as Bea drove along the car's gentle rocking made Ruth sleepy. Just before she nodded off, Murray yielded to the cradle effects of the car's motion, and his head fell against her shoulder. Ruth smiled and sat very still.

The Independence Day Parade

Friday, July 4, 1947 dawned bright and warm. By seven a.m. the thermometer reached seventy-six degrees under a calm blue sky and a relentless yellow sun, just clearing the oaks that lined Butler Street behind the courthouse. The Flournoys, the Lewises, the Armisteads and just about everyone else in the neighborhood were getting ready to go downtown to the Fourth of July parade. The Riverton High Marching Band would lead the Shriners, the Veterans of Foreign Wars, the American Legion, the Garden Club, and other organizations. The principal of the black high school had asked the mayor for permission to have their band, "The Strutting Cavaliers," march in the parade, but was refused. Some of the black children and parents grumbled among themselves about the rejection, but they did not press the mayor for an explanation.

By 9:00 a.m. both sides of Marshall Boulevard were lined with spectators. The parade would begin at 10:00 with Miss Riverton, the mayor, and the chief of police leading the procession in a convertible provided by Newton Cadillac. They would be dropped off at City Park, at the western end of Marshall, and take seats in the gazebo. There they would greet the marchers as they arrived in the park and took their seats on the grass or on the wooden benches fronting the gazebo. The parade began at the east end of Marshall, eight blocks away, on a side street next to the west side of the Blalock County Courthouse.

A little before ten, with the temperature rising, and everyone fanning themselves with cardboard fans, folded newspapers, or wide-brimmed hats, the mayor's car suddenly appeared from the side street and moved slowly down the boulevard toward the park. With Miss Riverton between them, seated on the top of the back seat, smiling and waving, the mayor and chief of police were also smiling and waving—-and thinking. The mayor wondered how many voters were in the crowd. He also thought about the heat: *I sure wish we could go faster and get a breeze in this car. I'll be glad when we can get in that gazebo under those shade trees.* The chief of police had similar thoughts. And he wondered if there were any lawbreakers in the crowd. The spectators were also smiling and waving and wishing they could get cooler. Some thought how nice it would be to duck into one of the air-conditioned shops, but all were closed for the holiday. The boys of Riverton had no complaints about the temperature because, like the Raiders and Renegades, they wore few clothes and were barefoot.

"Here comes His Highness," said Ruby Lewis, as she used her handkerchief to wipe the sweat from her slender neck. "He needs to be walkin' instead of ridin' in a Cadillac. I wonder how much the rental on that is costing the taxpayers?"

"I'm sure it's 'donated' by Larry Newton," said Raymond, who was fanning himself with his fedora panama hat. "You <u>know</u> Howard Duncan and Larry have some sort of a sweetheart deal worked out. During the war there was talk about how Larry's son Brad got his cushy stateside assignment because Howard headed up the draft board. And who knows what kind of deal was arranged when Blalock Mills got the war contract for the uniforms. I think the Chief was in on those deals also. He doesn't strike me as being smart enough to be Chief of Police of a city the size of Riverton."

Ruby could have added another, highly dramatic complaint to her husband's litany, but she didn't dare. She feared Raymond might kill the mayor and be sent to prison. Then where would she and the children be? The incident had occurred two years before during the VJ Day celebrations. They were at a Civitan dance where Howard Duncan had been drinking heavily and talking loudly. The efforts of his poor wife to calm him down were wasted, and she was getting quite embarrassed. When she went to the powder room, Howard asked Ruby to dance, and while they were dancing, Howard noticed Raymond on the other side of the room engaged in spirited conversation with some other men. Seeing both spouses occupied, he whispered a drooling invitation into Ruby's ear and let his right hand slide down to her buttocks. Ruby froze, and her anger surged upward. She felt a powerful urge to slap him but resisted. She simply pulled away and walked back to her table.

Ruby decided to add nothing to Raymond's remarks, so she just sighed and shielded her eyes as she looked up the boulevard for the first marchers.

Having little interest in the parade and still bothered by his UFO experience, Raymond raised his eyes and scanned the sky.

Marsha and Nathan Armistead were standing on either

side of a lamppost on the other side of the street, in front of
Boniface Drugs. Neither of them cared much for parades but
felt obligated to be there for appearance sake. Being seen
at the Fourth of July parade was *de rigeur* on the Riverton
social calendar. Unlike the Lewises, the Armisteads had been
raised in middle-class families and been imbued with social
aspirations, especially Marsha. They had taken this particular
spot on the parade route because Marsha hoped to be seen by
the right people. It was customary for Mrs. Howard Duncan,
Mrs. Larry Newton, Mrs. Bob Forrester, and other notables
to watch from the upstairs windows of the drug store. There
they could sit and enjoy the air conditioning Lou Boniface
would leave on for them. Some years the queen of Riverton
society, Mrs. Ray Pettigrew, would appear at one of the
windows and wave to the crowd below. Her husband was
the principal partner of the consortium which owned Blalock
Mills. Marsha would have been flabbergasted to learn she
was standing next to Ray's mistress, who was also looking
up at the windows.

Nathan wanted only to maintain whatever social
standing was necessary to do well in his business pursuits,
but Marsha burned to be included among the social elite.
She dreamed of sending Blake to Forrest Academy and Janie
to Flo Hennessy, but both were exclusive, quite expensive
private schools. There were also the balls. She ached to be

invited to Mystery Host or Sultans Soiree. And wouldn't it be "dee-<u>vine</u>" if Janie could be introduced at the Riverton Debutantes Ball. Thus, Marsha spent her time at the parade alternately looking out at the passing marchers and up at the windows of the drugstore. Nathan just gazed at the marchers while fanning himself with his panama hat.

When Ruth and Cousin Bea arrived at City Park, all of the benches facing the parade route had been taken. Upon seeing the elderly ladies approaching, a young couple offered them their bench and sat on the grass nearby.

"Bea, can you see the Scouts yet?" Ruth asked as they settled onto the bench.

"No, I think they're somewhere near the end, with the soldiers."

Ruth looked forward to the parade for the first time in many years. She wanted to be there to see Murray carry the American flag for his Boy Scout troop. It would thrill her to see Murray thus affirmed as a full-fledged American citizen in light of the depressing news of the day. The newspaper and magazine accounts of Nazi brutality toward Jews had greatly saddened her. She was ashamed of the so-called German Christians who had committed those unspeakable crimes, and she felt especially sorry for young Jews like Murray who would have to carry on after the horror of the genocide.

Murray adjusted well to Scouting. He made friends with several of the boys in his troop, and none of them seemed to care that he was a Jew. In fact, a couple of them wanted to know more about the faith, and about the nascent Jewish state of Israel. Murray remembered little of Rabbi Jacob's lessons, but he had learned a great deal from the books Ruth got him. He would also question his mother, and his inquiries made Sara very happy because she had been worried about Murray's commitment to his faith, but now he was asking all kinds of questions, showing more interest than ever before.

He especially enjoyed hearing her account of the heroic but vain defense of the Masada stronghold against a Roman onslaught and telling his Christian friends about that famous historic event.

Not long after Ruth and Bea sat down a convertible stopped and disgorged Howard and the Chief. Ruth looked over at the two men climbing the stairs of the gazebo.

"That Howard Duncan is too much like his father for my taste," said Ruth. "Rod Duncan fancied himself a ladies' man and wore the vilest cologne. He always talked loud, too. If he hadn't been such a smelly show-off, he would have been a nice looking young man."

"Yeah, I remember Rod. He was quite a bit older than me," replied Bea, "but I'll never forget how he would just barge right in and take over whenever he joined a group of his friends. He always acted like everybody was just bidin' their time until he could show up. I stayed away from him."

Ruth again looked up the boulevard, squinting against the sunlight, to see if she could see Murray and the Scouts.

"I sure hope Murray's parents are here to see him. I know he'll be handsome in his uniform. When I found out he got a faded, second-hand uniform, I got a brand new one and sent it to him. He'll be in high school soon. I better look into how his schoolwork is getting along. I'd like to see him lose some more weight, too. The hiking and camping he's done has slimmed him down some, but I'd like to see him lose some more. I wonder if he could go out for the football team next fall?"

"Ruth, you're sounding more and more like a grand-mother. Where did all this come from? You and Rachael never showed much interest in children, other than mine, of course. But now you're frettin' every day about a Jewish boy from the other side of town."

"Oh, I just feel sorry for him. He's at a critical time in his life and he needs a friend who understands. You were a little young to remember me when I was that age, Bea, but I was a lot like Murray, and I needed a friend, too."

The benches and lawn around the two ladies were rapidly filling up with marchers who had completed their march when Ruth saw a boy holding an American flag off in the distance. She couldn't see any facial features, but she was patient. She carefully cleaned her glasses with her handkerchief, and after a couple of minutes she could make out the handsome figure of Murray marching at the head of the Scout troops. As he became easier to see, her chest expanded, filling with a grandmother's pride. And when she could see the toothy grin on his freckled face, a smile spread across her carefully powdered, wrinkled face.

Priscilla Andrews was standing with Anne Bonair halfway along the parade route. Although she didn't much care for standing in oppressive heat and watching a parade, she wanted to set a good example for her students. In her civics lessons she stressed the importance of patriotism. And when she talked about citizenship she always made it a point to include "colored" people. She was careful to avoid seditious remarks about the Jim Crow laws, which could get her fired, but as an educator she was determined to convey to her pupils that blacks are citizens, too.

Fanning herself with her red straw hat with a blue and white band, Priscilla said, "Anne, wouldn't it be nice if we could have the Fourth of July sometime in March?"

"Sure would."

"Those Founding Fathers were crazy for convening in July to draft the Declaration of Independence. Even up north in Philadelphia it gets hot in the summer, and they spent several days in a stuffy room without benefit of air conditioning or even electric fans. Women would have had more sense. They would have met outside under a shade tree next to a lake and made a picnic out of it. Being more comfortable the women would have produced a document that was less harsh. All that tough language I'm sure was due to the men suffering from the heat."

"They should have just taken off all their clothes," Ann replied. "That way we would have gotten the Naked Truth: 'We hold these Naked Truths to be self-evident...'" Both women laughed at the mental image of Naked Founders, as they continued fanning themselves.

"Anne, do you recognize that boy carrying the American flag?"

"Yes, he's the Jewish boy I had a couple of years ago. Good pupil. Smart. But he seemed to get in a lot of scrapes with the other children. I did what I could to help him get along with the other boys, but I'm afraid he never did get accepted. He sure looks accepted now. And he makes a dashing figure in his uniform. He wasn't so handsome before. I'm tickled he's doing so well. Maybe I can catch him after the speech and talk to him."

"I didn't have that boy, but I do remember him on the playground and in the hallways," Priscilla added. "I always felt sorry for him and gave him a kind word whenever I could."

Priscilla wanted to talk to Anne about her conversations with Gayle Freemont, but she didn't dare. Even though they were good friends and colleagues, Anne was definitely Old South and might not appreciate her activities. She didn't want to risk their friendship and collegiality if Anne were unsympathetic. It mystified Priscilla how discriminatory the whites could be toward their black fellow citizens, with whom they associated daily. This was brought out most dramatically during the war when German POWs on their way to the Army base were fed in the train depot's nice dining room, while black American soldiers had to eat at a dingy diner across the street. She felt sure such ludicrous situations had prompted the recent integration of the armed forces.

I wonder if Gayle served during the war, Priscilla thought, as she shielded her eyes against the glare of the sun. Even before the last of the marchers passed by their spot in the parade route, Priscilla had grown weary of the pomp and circumstance and begun reflecting on her life.

Colored people aren't the only ones discriminated against. I don't understand why women weren't invited to the convention in Philadelphia. I know it's a man's world and men are supposed to make all the important decisions, but I don't understand why. In many instances a woman's input could have made situations better. I also don't like the different standards of beauty between men and women. Why is gray hair "distinguished" on men and not on women? Of course, my acne scars would be repulsive on both men and women, but here again, why? "Beauty is only skin deep, but ugly goes to the bone," as the saying goes. Beneath my ugly skin I am a beautiful person, if I have to say so myself. Gayle is a rather handsome young man, but he's colored. Guess we both have a "skin" problem.

Gayle Freemont was standing with the other "colored" people near the start of the parade near Butler Street. He was with Justina Holliday from the college, watching the high school bands pass by, the trumpets blaring, and the drums booming. Occasionally a sour note would emerge from a clarinet or cornet. Wondering about the difference between these white bands and black ones, Justina asked, "Gayle, do you think these white high school bands are better than our bands?"

"No...I think they're about the same," Gayle said. "The main difference it seems to me is that the white bands look like they're leadin' a funeral procession, compared to Negro bands. White people don't know how to let loose and enjoy life. My grandfather used to tell me that if a white man could be a Negro for one Saturday night he wouldn't want to be a white man anymore. I think there's a lot of truth in that. We think they lack passion, and they think we have too much."

"I don't think I agree with you," Justina responded. "My mother told me when I was a little girl never to give a white man any encouragement to 'be friendly' as she put it then. She said they will take advantage of a Negro girl. So I would say that indicates a lot of passion."

Taking off his straw hat and wiping his forehead with his handkerchief, Gayle replied, "Justina, I don't think it is so much passion as it is lack of respect. Some white men think that all Negroes have no morals. They think that because we are so quick to laugh and so uninhibited in our behavior that we don't exercise any moral constraint. What I mean to say is those men equate constraint with morality. If you let yourself go and enjoy yourself you must be immoral. I've seen it myself a few times. I'll be in the company of a white man I barely know and he will ask personal questions about my sex life. He assumes all Negroes cheat on their wives or husbands. We certainly have our share of those kinds of people—-maybe more than our share-—but it's not fair to condemn the rest of us."

Shielding her eyes with her hand as she surveyed a river of white people passing by in the parade, Justina said, "That's just one more big issue we'll have to deal with down the road."

Pete Flournoy had some urgent office work to do, so he dropped off Anna and Susan near the parade route and continued on to his office. Graham, Todd and Blake had ridden to town on their bicycles. It was the first time they had been allowed to ride so far from home, and Anna was a little worried.

"Mama, let's find a shady spot," Susan said as they approached the parade route.

"That's a great idea, Susan, but if we stand under one of the store awnings we can't see the parade through the crowds lining the street."

"What about taking a seat upstairs at Boniface Drugs?" Susan teased.

Frowning playfully at her middle daughter, Anna replied, "The family of the county school superintendent doesn't have enough social standing for that privilege. It would be nice to sit in that cool room, but I don't think I would enjoy exchanging pleasantries with the likes of Mrs. Ray Pettigrew."

"I think you're just jealous, Mama."

"I don't think so, child. It would pain me if any of you girls grew up to be nothing more than a social butterfly. I'm very pleased that Marsha has become a teacher. And I'm also pleased about your ambition to be a marine scientist, or whatever you call it. I didn't get to go to college myself, but your Granny and Granddaddy valued education and helped me as much as they could."

Susan had grown tired of the conversation and was scanning the high school band to see if Roy Dunlevy was marching. She was interested in Roy because, like her, he was interested in science. He was thinking about applying to M.I.T. but was afraid his grades weren't good enough. Sometimes Susan and Roy would meet at the Carnegie Library and study together. Even though he was a serious student, he liked pop music and could do a great imitation of Vaughn Monroe. Just the week before when they were having sodas at Topper's Drugstore and Soda Fountain, Roy got out of their booth, faced all of the kids in the other booths and, in a fake baritone, with arms outstretched, began, "Dance, bal-le-ri-na, dance/ And do your pi-ro-uette in rhythm with your a-ching heart..." Laughter, wolf whistles and derisive imitations from the other teenagers followed his performance. Some of the girls faked a swoon.

Anna spotted a space on the corner of Marshall and Lindbergh and pulled Susan into it. Susan continued to look for the boy, and Anna began looking up and down the sidewalk for Graham, getting a little worried about the trouble the boys might get into.

"Boy! I sure wish I could have one of those M-1s," said Blake, as he, Graham and Todd ran alongside the National Guard unit marching in the parade. Sporting blue lanyards, polished silver helmets, white leggings, and white gloves, the Precision Drill Team of the Guard was doing synchronized moves with their rifles. Behind them the rest of the unit marched in perfect formation. The three boys had waited for the unit to come around the corner at the courthouse and had followed them down Marshall Boulevard. They didn't care much for the rest of the marchers.

"Man, look at those snappy rifle flips!" said Todd, as he stopped and pushed his way to the front of the crowd.

"I can't wait 'til I'm old enough to join," said Graham, as he pushed in behind him, mimicking the leg and hand movements of the drill team. He accidentally struck a middle-aged man standing next to him, and the man scowled at all three boys.

"Look!" cried Blake. "There's Murray!" Murray had worked so hard learning how to march with the flag that he had been chosen to lead the Scouts in the parade. A phone call from Ruth had helped. He was bursting with pride and stepping high, resplendent in his new uniform. His cap was angled perfectly on his head. It was neither "country hick" nor rakish. His reddish hair was neatly trimmed and he wore a bright smile. All in all he made a handsome figure.

"Man, I wish I wuz a Boy Scout!" offered Todd.

"You could be a Cub Scout now, dummy," Graham replied. "You gotta be twelve to be a Boy Scout."

Pushing himself in front of his friends so he could see the passing Scouts better, Blake asked, "Do you think Murray will fight in the chinaberry battle next summer?"

Graham and Todd looked toward the receding figure of Murray and replied, simultaneously, plaintively, "Naw, I don't think so." With that said, the boys pushed back from the crowd and ran toward the park to catch up with the Guardsmen. As they ran past the Scouts and then the Guardsmen, Todd imagined his future. He would be a Scout- -an Eagle Scout--and then a National Guard General and get decorated for winning battles overseas, and then ride in a Cadillac convertible at the head of the parade, and then give the Fourth of July speech in the City Park.

Graham's thoughts were about the people they were dodging as they ran along the crowded sidewalk, weaving in and out. He had always been interested in people. He wanted to get to the park and get a good seat for the speech. Blake liked the marching, the rhythmic, synchronized motion. He liked the bright colors and the loud, brassy music. He loved a colorful parade more than ice cream.

Graham got to the park first, and Todd got there a short time later. Blake stopped to watch the Guardsmen complete their march but caught up when Todd yelled at him. All three boys knew exactly where to go for the best seat: the oak in the southeast corner of the park. They climbed up the lower branches and sat down on a large limb ten feet above ground. The stout limb was parallel to the front of the gazebo, so they could sit facing the speaker and see just fine. The only drawback to their perch was that ants would crawl along the limb and go inside their short pants. They had learned two years before not to let go of the limb to slap with both hands. The first time it happened to Blake, he slapped with both hands, lost his grip and fell on a man standing under the tree. Fortunately, when Blake yelled the man looked up and was able to catch him.

Now the boys were fully content. They had seen a great parade, were seated on their limb, and, best of all, they could savor their stunning victory in their first chinaberry battle with the Ramar Renegades. Their thoughts about the battle made their chests swell with pride.

The general hubub of the crowd slowly subsided as Mayor Howard Duncan tapped on the microphone and yelled "Testing!" three times over screeching static from the speakers. After the crowd quieted down, Howard took off his linen suit coat and loosened his tie so he would look more like a man of the people. Then he moved to the microphone with what he hoped was a manly stroll.

"My fellow citizens, white and COLORED!" He shouted "colored" to make sure the black citizens sitting at the back in folding chairs could hear him. "We have a lot to be thankful for on July 4, 1947. Life is looking good. Our loved ones are back from the war, and they have good jobs. In fact, I see even more good jobs on the horizon." Here he paused to let that sink in. "Blalock Mills expects to start hirin' real soon. Mr. Pettigrew is lookin' to get a big guvmint contract to make military apparel, and Marsten Army Depot will be hirin' soon. They need more civilian help for a big manpower increase in the next few months. This new guvmint spendin' will mean that cash registers all over Riverton will be playin' our favorite song—-the sound of money!" This attempt at humor generated a scattered, low-level laughter.

A little disappointed at the weak response to his humor, Howard continued, "Why is the guvmint spendin' more on the military, you ask?" Because of the Russians, my friends. We've got to stay ahead of the Russians if we hope to avoid a Third World Wah. Right now we are the only country with the atom bum, and we gotta keep it that way! And us havin' a strong, vigilant defense can keep 'em from gettin' it! As a God-fearin' people we have God on our side, and that means the godless Russians can't win! So don't forget to thank God as we go about our day-to-day bidness!

"Another fly in the buttermilk for Riverton is outsiders meddlin' in our affairs. They want to destroy our time-honored Southern traditions and the racial harmony we enjoy. They talk about integratin' the schools, the restaurants, and all such as that."

"Booo!" rang out from several of the white men and some of the white women.

"What I want to know is, How do they know what's best for our community when they don't live here? From where I sit, the coloreds and the whites are gittin' along jus' fine, and everybody is content with our 'separate but equal' way uh life. I don't know of any coloreds who are unhappy, and I don't think you do either! As mayor I travel to all parts of the city and talk to all kinds of people, and I can tell you that your friends and neighbors are happy with the way things are." A few cheers and whistles rang out from the white audience. The black citizens just sat there, mute and dignified. Both Gayle and Justina wanted to say something but resisted, as did Priscilla in the white section.

Prompted by the mayor's remarks, the three boys began thinking about the future:

Blake: *One day I will march in the Fourth of July parade. I'll wear a solid white uniform with a red cape. I'll have a bright blue hat with a white feather in front. My trumpet will be the loudest of all the instruments. All the other marchers will be behind me. I'll lead the circus parade. Clyde Beatty will march beside me poppin' his whip, and the elephants will be behind us blastin' their trunks. My trumpet will be louder than the elephants. Way in the back will be the lions roarin'.*

Todd: *If those Russians attack I'll lead an army of tanks. They'll be loaded with atom bums. I'll be standin' in a jeep in front of the tanks. No! I'll be standin' on my motorcycle. I'll be lookin' backward at the tanks. The silver stars on my shoulders are shinin'. My silver helmet is shinin'. My right arm is held up. I draw it forward and ride off on my Indian Chief and all the tanks rumble behind me.*

Graham: *The mayor said that he doesn't know any unhappy colored people. But what about that colored man I saw on the bus with those colored women? He sure didn't look happy sittin' back there with those yappin' old colored women. And what about Ruthelle? She didn't want to talk about the schools. Neither did Miz Ruth. I wouldn't mind goin' to school with Crayton. That was fun talkin' to him. And I want to know more about the Negro baseball league. All those people in front of the mayor are white. The colored are all in the back. I wonder if one day they will be mixed together? . . . And what if the mayor is a colored man?!!*

"In conclusion, the mayor continued, "I would just like to say that the future for Riverton is as bright as today's sunshine." At the mention of the sun, a few whites and blacks looked toward the sun-drenched street outside the shady park but quickly looked back when the sunlight hurt their eyes. "We have racial harmony and bidness is good and lookin' better, so we can look forward to many years of peace and prosperity!...Thank you for your kind attention!"

The audience applauded politely. Howard bowed and turned to shake the hand of the Chief of Police and kiss the cheek of Miss Riverton. The audience stood up to visit friends and neighbors seated close by.

The boys jumped down from the tree and ran to get their bicycles. As they rode along, the playing cards in their spokes *brapped* loudly. Blake asked what "peace and prosperity" means, and in the discussion that followed the boys decided they had it already. They had decisively won the chinaberry battle and were having the best summer of their lives.

"Last one home is a rotten egg!" Graham shouted and took off in a flash, pedaling madly. Todd and Blake followed in hot pursuit. Soon the King of Diamonds, the King of Hearts, and the Joker were shrieking and the boys were streaking down sidewalks, along dirt road side streets, and between houses in a frantic race. Each boy wanted to be first to climb the tree and flop himself on the floor of the tree house, which was now the official home of the 1947 Chinaberry Battle Champions.

2019 ✓
2020 ✓
2021 ✓ ✓ ✓

Printed in the United States
59031LVS00004B/103-150

9 781425 943035